Valley
of the
Sorcerers

Valley of the Sorcerers

A NOVEL BY
KAMAL ABDULLA

TRANSLATED FROM AZERBAIJANI BY ANNE THOMPSON

Strategic Book Publishing and Rights Co.

Strategic Book Publishing and Rights Co.
12620 FM 1960, Suite A4-507
Houston, TX 77065
www.sbpra.com

For information about special discounts for bulk purchases,
please conttact   Strategic Book Publishing and Rights Co.
Special Sales, at bookorder@sbpra.net

ISBN: 978-1-63135-343-7

Book Design by Julius Kiskis

21 22 20 19 18 17 16 15 14   2 3 4 5 6

Dedication

Everyone has a valley of the sorcerers and longs for it
throughout their lives, sometimes consciously, sometimes
unconsciously. Those who unconsciously long for the valley
will pass this book by. It is dedicated to them . . .

Contents

The Caravanbashi, searching for the spirit of his father, Mammadqulu the Headsman, is drawn to the Valley of the Sorcerers. Sayyah the Sorcerer, a disciple of the White Dervish, tries to summon the spirit. The Caravanbashi's mysterious meeting with the spirit is to end in tragedy.

Preface

The Valley of the Sorcerers by contemporary Azerbaijani author Kamal Abdulla is a work of fiction born of the influence of Sufism, an important component of medieval and subsequent Islamic culture or, to put it in modern terminology, the main trend in medieval Islamic philosophy and literature. It is an important culturological trend, which shaped Islamic philosophy, poetry and music of the Middle Ages and has an influence on contemporary culture to this day.

At that time literature was the literature of all Muslim peoples – Arab tribes, Turkic-speaking (including Azerbaijani) and Persian-speaking peoples, although elements of classical Islamic literature are present in the poetry of peoples who were drawn into the Islamic world, such as, for example, the Spanish-born Jewish poet and philosopher, Judah Ha-Levi.

At the root of Sufism is purification through thought. Purification is present in one form or another in all world religions. Shintoism is translated as the path (in the philosophical sense of path or study) of the gods, Buddhism as the enlightened (awakened or enlightened teacher), Islam by the consonants s-l-m – wholeness or peace, Zoroaster as sparkling star or "fire or star" that is contemplated while the main deity of Zoroastrianism is Ahura (or Ormizd) Mazda (Wise Lord). All teachings are thus linked with the enlightenmint that comes through instruction . . .

All the wisdom of the Creator – Lord of the World – Wise Man – Teacher is passed on to mankind. Gradually this function of the holy scriptures – the passing on of wisdom – is transferred to books written by people too.

This book is no exception.

The novel could be considered as contemporary Sufi novel, representing blurring borders of real and transcendental world. The Sufis have various ways of attaining wisdom. The main one is how to remember God (zikr) and attain his perfection, which is possible through cutting oneself off from the real world. The path to comprehension described in the novel is vird (for the author this is a time of unity with God). Vird is the cyclical turning of the zikr, one of the Sufi rituals. As well as the cyclicality of movement, vird is also the understanding of the wholeness of the world through its cyclicality, circularity.

The cinematographic novel Valley of the Sorcerers erases the border between temporal strata – past and present, mystical and real, stitching them evenly with a single needle so that they turn into Ariadne's thread. To some extent, this is not even a needle but a pin. In the role of a needle – the motif of revenge – as old as this world; in the role of pin – the closed circle, or to be more exact the life path of man, the time given to him for a worthy life, which the author cyclically recalls. Time here is neither the mystical-utopian chronotope of the dervishes from the eternally green Valley of the Sorcerers nor the real present and past of the characters.

The closed circles – paths of all the characters beat out a rhythm among themselves, coming together in a spiral around that Vengeance, which, as a destructive stimulus for the actions of the characters from the diachrony of real time, draws them to celebrate justice; an action that stumbles on that stone in the act of searching for the truth.

The characters of the mystical-utopian world of the dervishes (who for the Sufis are analogous to the clergy in other religions, while in this novel the dervishes have the role of sorcerers) from the eternally green valley, inspired by Sufi traditions, or the spirit of the ancestors summoned to the present (the father – headsman), as in Shakespeare's Hamlet and in part for the same reason, called to help in the search for truth, are unable to stop the invincible passion of vengeance as a supposed victory. In this way the finale of the novel becomes the end of a circle, which must inevitably be repeated by the son of the Caravanbashi.

But in this tragic, seemingly hopeless finale, the successor to the unjustly accused apprentice to the Teacher, manages to lead the newly orphaned child out of the labyrinth of malice, saving his soul in his Valley: only the residents of the Valley of the Sorcerers have the new life of migrated souls, not vengeful and bloody because of revenge, but meditative.

We hope that his novel will be a bridge of culture between the eternal question of revenge, the cyclicality of life and the human life path, independent of religion, denomination and nationality.

Rahilya Geybullayeva

Chapter 1

Into the Valley of the Sorcerers

I f he just stretched out his hand, he could touch them. Lost in wonder yet again, the Caravanbashi[1] contemplated the tired, mischievous stars sprinkled like salt right above his head. A while later he turned his gaze to the mules, camels, and horses that had found themselves a spot for the night. Breathing heavily, the caravan sank into the silence of the night. The snuffling of the camels and whinnying of the horses, snuggled down into the dry earth, mingled with the distant howling of dogs and wolves, stirred a sense of unease in the human listener, akin to meeting a stranger on the road. Nothing else disturbed the ominous calm. Here and there campfires burnt themselves out like the day, leaving glowing embers. The camels, horses, and mules lay still as stones covered in moss in their earthen beds. This is how the large caravan of animals, servants, slaves, and camel drivers laid up for the night.

After a long, exhausting journey, the caravan was almost at

---

1 The Caravanbashi is the head of a caravan, a train of horses, camels, and mules carrying goods.

the border of its own land. The Caravanbashi could sense that when the frozen ground slowly changed to more familiar hues. Inshallah, God willing, when they reached their own land, they need no longer be afraid of robbers. Although there wasn't far to go, fear still lay like a rotting corpse out in the fields. He watched with satisfaction as three tall, dark figures walked side by side from one end of the camp to the other—they were the watchmen. He knew each of them well and trusted them. These weren't empty words. Back home they had come through a thousand and one trials before he had agreed to let them join his caravan.

As the watchmen drew closer they gave no sign of knowing him and, following the rules, asked him the name of the night. And what would you do with me if I didn't know? the Caravanbashi thought to himself, but out loud he said, "The dark red horizon." The watchmen moved on, melting into the darkness.

Every night had its own name, which was invented early every morning by the Caravanbashi's most trusted man, Khaja Ibrahim Agha[2]. The name was spread amongst the people of the caravan, and they alone knew it. This was how the caravan protected itself on the long and terrible journey. Protection from robbers and thieves, bandits and brigands, was really important. It was no laughing matter—the caravan was a beloved lady bedecked in jewels and fine garments who was to be cast beforethe Pivot of the Universe.[3] Only then would the goods destined for the bazaar be sent there, and the goods ordered by customers be delivered to them.

He had led this type of caravan many times now. It was easy for him to travel, as if fate had quietly written this into his destiny. Back at home, his wife, son, and servants matured, advanced in

---

2 The title Khaja was applied to eunuchs.

3 "Pivot of the Universe" was one of the titles used to refer to the shah of Iran.

years, and grew older as they waited for him, while he never changed. It was as though a strange force, a current, had shot through all seven layers of his self[4] and kept him in a state of tension. He could not grow old in any way, could not even wear himself out. He'd had a higher mission, a holy mystery, from his earliest days—or maybe not. He could not know for sure.

Not wanting to weary his brain with any more philosophy, the Caravanbashi went into the tent specially erected for him. Khaja Ibrahim Agha appeared out of the darkness and followed him inside. This khaja was a red-bearded man. Each bristle of his beard seemed to be redder than ever. His face won't have seen a drop of water for a month, thought the Caravanbashi. The sooner we get home onto our turf, into our own houses, the better. These poor devils are exhausted, he thought sadly as he took a candle from the corner, lit it with a flint, and stood it on a copper tray.

A menacing half-light filtered through the tent, casting shadows. The Caravanbashi turned his sorrowful face towards Ibrahim. "What is it? What do you want?"

Ibrahim's heart lurched. "Sir, I've come . . . my heart was uneasy, there's not far to go. We just have to cross the pass ahead of us and then we'll be in the valley."

"I know. Are you trying to teach me the way?"

"No sir, I know you are uneasy too. May this job finish soon, inshallah. I came to see if you need me for anything? Shall I massage your feet?"

"No, Ibrahim, you go and get some rest. We're all really tired today." The Caravanbashi narrowed his eyes. "What do you think? Maybe they won't be in the valley?"

"No, unfortunately they are always there, but I don't know about ours. I am really hopeful, but . . . what can we know? They stand all along the valley. That is what they do if no one comes

---

4 The Sufi believe there are seven levels of the self.

and gives them work."

"There's not long to go now. God willing, the person we need will be among them."

"He will, he will. You can be sure of that, don't worry. We put our trust in Almighty God."

"Amen. Off you go. I'm going to snatch some sleep if I can."

Walking backwards, Ibrahim left the warm tent for the cold night air. Outside, the light that glittered from every star seemed to reach the earth, flooding the land with daylight. An ethereal sound of touching lamentation seemed to emanate from the light. Ibrahim looked around and moved closer to the tent. The camel, Qotazli, was settled on the ground, his flank rising and falling rhythmically. Nazarali, the camel boy, was fast asleep, his head resting on Qotazli's flank. Ibrahim chose a spot on the other flank, took something like a kilim from the camel, stamped the earth to soften it, spread out the rug, and lay down on it. He tossed from side to side and softened the ground a bit more, but couldn't get to sleep no matter what he did. Gazing at the mischievous, tired stars up in the sky, he plunged deep in thought.

The name of the valley that Ibrahim had just been talking about with the Caravanbashi was the Valley of the Sorcerers. The valley opened up where Snake Pass ended, and the green sward began at the foot of what was known as the Invisible Mountain. The valley had been given its name because they believed that every famous sorcerer from the Maghreb to the Middle East chose this place to live. Why they chose this spot, no one knew. They themselves did not say a word about it. Throughout the valley you could see the sorcerers—alone or in pairs—gathered together taking a stroll, waving their arms, talking to one another, or staying silent.

The road that passed through the valley was the main source of life for the sorcerers. They hoped for alms and gifts from wayfarers and received enough to get by. Sometimes a wayfarer took one of the sorcerers away to use his help with magic. When the wayfarer got what he wanted, he developed faith in the sorcerer's miraculous powers. His miraculous work completed, the sorcerer returned to his place in the Valley of the Sorcerers, and only when he had reached the foot of a half-buried, half-bare rock known only to him, would he breathe freely.

The sorcerers had a rule that anyone who brought back earnings share them with everyone. It was impossible for a returning sorcerer not to share his earnings with the others; they shared their food and drink, their joys and sorrows, their travels, they talked together, and kept silent together.

Each day, every sorcerer stole away to spend an hour or two alone behind a rock or perhaps one of the thorny, bushy shrubs, tall as trees, known only to them. This was known as the time of solitude. It was a sacred time for them. No sorcerer dared approach another at that time; to do so was forbidden. What the sorcerer did, or did not do, during that time he alone knew. He talked to himself in a language that no one else knew. He asked himself questions and answered them too. It was impossible to know the language.

However, one of the sorcerers who had been taken to the city by a god-fearing merchant to cast a spell on his neighbour for heaping a thousand and one troubles on his head, in the heat of the moment once revealed the secret of the time of solitude. He said that every sorcerer stripped himself of his magic during that time. He was left weak and defenceless as a child. They entrusted their magic to someone or something. When they emerged from the time of solitude, whatever had happened was forgotten.

This god-fearing merchant was later tempted by the gold and silver he had paid to the sorcerer who revealed the secret; he regretted the loss of the money and decided to spy on the sorcerer. He planned to follow him and get the money back when the time of solitude came. He began to spy on the sorcerer. When the hour came and the sorcerer entered his time of solitude, he covered his eyes with his hands, stood ramrod straight behind his usual rocks, and paid heed to nothing. The merchant appeared at that moment. Without saying a word, he began to search the sorcerer's garments, rummaging through his pockets. The frail sorcerer could not stop him. The man found the money he had given. He saw the gold wrapped in a blue rag, took it, and crammed it into his pockets, taking to his heels away from the area of solitude.

Although he shouldn't have done it, the merchant couldn't resist turning back to look at the sorcerer's face. His eyes closed and an offended smile on his lips, the sorcerer said, "Go, but I do not consider this money honestly earned; it is not halal."

The man paid no heed to these words. He scurried up to the road leading out of the valley to the city and set out breathlessly for home. It was the same road and the city stood in its place. It's hard to believe that the desperate man is walking along the treacherous path to this day and the road will not let him go. He walks around and around the Invisible Mountain, and somehow ends up again close to Snake Pass at the head of the valley. People have followed him but cannot understand how this man who knows the road so well can get so lost, and how he can keep walking, disappear from view, and end up behind the person following him—mystery of mysteries.

There are those who tell quite a different story. They say that the god-fearing merchant has become an old man, has been earning his livelihood in his hometown, and continues to do so to this day. They say that he never came to these parts, never took a sorcerer from the foot of the Invisible Mountain, and his ignoble neighbours are in rude health, hale and hearty, living in their own homes. God's mystery? Of course, God's mystery!

Ibrahim and the Caravanbashi had good reason to be anxious as they headed into the Valley of the Sorcerers—they planned to choose a sorcerer to take away with them. They were not looking for a run-of-the-mill sorcerer. It was important that he have more than a special talent for sorcery and magic. Inshallah, fate willed that the Caravanbashi would at last fulfil an ancient mystery, a plan long cherished in his heart. Ibrahim shared his beloved Caravanbashi's great desire for the plan to come to fruition. Each passing day he saw the body of the Caravanbashi creak and groan from its tribulations, and suffered even more than him. In his ravaged heart he asked God to bring a rapid end to this suffering.

The Caravanbashi's secret wish was to summon the spirit of his father, Mammadqulu the Headsman, who many years ago had gone mad and left for a life in the wilds. He passed away, leaving no trace and no grave. His son had never seen him properly. The Caravanbashi wanted to talk to him, to ask his father some questions. The wretched Caravanbashi needed a sorcerer to make his wish come true. Ibrahim gave a confident pledge that they would find a spirit-summoning sorcerer in the valley and take him with them. If they did not, then the Caravanbashi's days would be even more torturous.

Khaja Ibrahim Agha could not say when he fell into a restless sleep, pondering this.

Chapter 2

The Headsman's Decision

Everything lay behind a tulle curtain; that's where things happened, if they happened at all. The Shah's faithful servant, the gleamingly moustachioed headsman Mammadqulu, never thought over his boldest moves, but with a nod in the direction of the Almighty plunged into action. Thinking that it would be easy, he behaved in exactly the same way with this journey. Though he thought he had plenty of time left, he summoned all his strength in mind and body. If he, whose every cell roared in motion, was surprised by his sudden decision, he should have been more discouraged than anyone.

What was this? You thought you were transported like a small child wandering off the path, or they took you from that path. You slept, you woke up suddenly, and you rubbed your knee with your ever-itchy hand. "Enough," you said. "I'm tired," you said. You didn't want anything other than to live out your days in the little crooked house, in the crooked, cobbled street in that beautiful city on the mountaintop in touching distance of the moon, a solitary cloud in the blue sky above.

So he took his decision, but for some reason a strange anxiety plucked at his heart strings, pulling them taut. The unease started an ache in his heart. Whatever it was, this ache appeared afresh.

8

When it began, his brain was drying out, as though he was hiding in multi-coloured mists. He grew numb, as though he had forgotten everything, and however hard he tried, no matter what he did, he could not find the strength within him to remember anything or anyone. This alone he knew distinctly—if he could remember someone or something, the pain turning quietly into an ache, as though rocked in the embrace of the black clouds, the stupor in his head would immediately pass; it would. To return to life from this terrible pain was a sweet dream for him.

Look at the works of God, he thought. He needed it now more than ever, for this punishment from the heavens—he could find no other name for it but punishment—this torment could not be described as a prize. No, this punishment came down to him from the heavens like a bird settling alone on its native bough. This affection, this love, this meaninglessness, which he never believed in before, never admitted to his consciousness because he had never encountered it, though he had heard a great deal about it, really was sweet suffering. Oh, God!

Maybe this girl loved him so much out of fear. Many who were afraid of him had all involuntarily sworn their love and lavished him with sweet promises, but as soon as he lay with each of them, he saw the barbs deep in their eyes. Whether from fear or revulsion, they wanted to throw him off like a blanket.

Trying to understand this fear in each of them, he said to himself, "No, this is not how it should be. If this is love, then I don't need it at all. The sooner it's over and this alien daughter of an alien man is out of my head, the better."

When he thought this, he could not finish what he was doing. Exhausted, he would half-finish the job and suddenly rise from the girl, who trembled from passion or fear, and start to get dressed, grumbling and swearing to himself. This is truly how it was, because Mammadqulu the Headsman hated people who were afraid of him.

Now, everything seemed different. This time there was no fear; this young bride didn't turn her gaze away from him. Shamelessly, she fixed her green eyes on him, not blinking her long lashes, and looked steadily at him. Not a sliver of separation remained between them. There was not a sliver of doubt that they had joined not just their trembling bodies but their trembling souls. They both understood that whatever this was, whatever had happened up until this point, was nothing but nonsense and vain chatter for them. Whatever happened afterwards belonged to the future.

It was on one of these nights that Mammadqulu the Headsman came to his fateful decision. The first amongst the executioners, the magnificently moustachioed Mammadqulu was carried by the army from state to state, city to city, nourished and cherished. Strapping, imposing, and broad shouldered as he approached his fiftieth year, he said to himself one day when he was feeling good, "I am God's servant; that's who I am!" Without forethought, without further ado, Mammadqulu the Headsman took his unexpected decision on the instruction of his soul.

This was his decision. In the city on the mountaintop, which is therefore closer to the heavens, stars, moon, and the one and only God, he would forever take his leave of this army, of the Padishah who had always shown him mercy, of his Vizier Mashdali, to whom he would never be able to repay his debt. He would throw himself at his feet; if necessary he would sob with tears pouring from his eyes like dark rain. "I am your servant until the day I die," he would sob to the amazed vizier.

If only he could find his tongue before the Padishah. If he could grant my humble request that he pardon me for straying from the path. "I entrust my only son to you," I would say. "Be a father to him as you have to me. I will remain here; I don't have the strength to go back. I am ending my service here; absolve me of my sins, Pivot of the Universe. Absolve me of my sins, you whose command I am leaving. I who arrived with you, but am not going back with you, either cut me in two, a mean traitor, or allow me to make my home in this city. I am so tired, oh Lord. I am impossibly tired."

This is how he begged Vizier Mashdali and, hanging his disobedient head, he would walk backwards out of the room, and return to the quiet, crooked street cobbled with river stones that start at the Multi-Coloured Mountain and ends no one knows where. He would return to this familiar street. Mammadqulu considered his service to his dearly beloved Padishah finished at this moment. What he had been counting on so impatiently was already over, but the invisible hand of fate had just started to count.

CHAPTER 3

The Invisible Mountain

With much hustle and bustle, the caravan was ready to leave. Everyone was in their place waiting for the order to set off. Only the Caravanbashi's tent was dark in the growing light of dawn. Ibrahim glanced once more at the well-laden camels and mules, the patient horsemen, and the three servants raking over the ashes of a large campfire near the tent as they waited for him.

Clearing his throat at the mouth of the tent, he bowed his head and gingerly entered. "Good morning, sir; we're ready."

Already in his travelling clothes, the Caravanbashi was sitting cross-legged on the still-warm bed, thinking. As soon as heard the expected words from Ibrahim, he leapt to his feet and straightened his crumpled clothes. "Very good, very good. Travellers should be on the road, and a good morning to you too. Have the tent taken down."

Ibrahim followed the Caravanbashi out of the tent. He gave a sign to the servants putting out the campfire to quickly pack the bedding and crockery inside the tent and load it onto the mules.

The Caravanbashi's thoroughbred horse was led out and he mounted it in a single leap. Ibrahim got on his horse too. A red-headed rider galloped up from the head of the caravan. Dismounting, he asked, "Agha, what are your orders?" This was his chief assistant, camel driver Qarasuvarli.

"Let's go, Qara," said the Caravanbashi decisively, looking over his shoulder at the still-dark road.

"Which road shall we take?" Qarasuvarli asked.

"The one that passes the foot of the Invisible Mountain."

"Through the Valley of the Sorcerers?"

"Yes, that way."

A muscle twitched almost imperceptibly on Qarasuvarli's face. A coolness slipped to his face from the depths of his eyes and melted into the air. He thought in his heart, May God keep us. Without saying another word, he turned his horse around and galloped back to the head of the caravan. He went ahead of the lead camels and gave the sign by raising his hand. The bugler gave a joyful blow on his horn. The hullaballoo increased and the caravan moved slowly and heavily on its way, a strange parting from the trees and fields around. Soon the camp was deserted; even the glowing embers of the campfires had breathed their last.

In one more day and night they would reach the main city. The road winding around the foot of the Invisible Mountain wasn't the only road in these parts. Many travellers had carved out a new road, and only those who wanted the services of a sorcerer still took the old road through the Valley of the Sorcerers. Otherwise, no wayfarer liked to take that road, and especially not a caravan. Nothing but fear entered people's souls there.

At the head of the caravan, Qotazli the camel majestically raised his snout and walked up to Qarasuvarli's horse. He took a further step in front, turned to the right, and vanished. Qarasuvarli disappeared with him, too. Ibrahim, who had been keeping his eye on Qotazli from a distance, galloped up to the Caravanbashi.

"May I bear your sorrows? Look, we've arrived but I cannot see Qotazli anymore."

Squinting his eyes as hard as he could, the Caravanbashi could not see Qotazli, and as he looked, the camels, horses, and mules in the long, twisting caravan disappeared one by one.

"Oh God, thank you for your wisdom. Look at the mysterious mountain and you can see nothing, but look the other way and you can see whatever is there," Ibrahim said to himself, trying to dispel the fear that stole into his soul.

Camels, mules, and horses passed the Invisible Mountain one by one. The tail of the caravan had already passed the mountain, and nothing could be seen of the caravan. A person could keep on looking but would not see a mountain or anything that lay in that direction, big or small.

Down to the left of the mountain opened up the gigantic void of the Valley of the Sorcerers. The Caravanbashi could hear the thumping of his heart in his temples. He almost drove two holes into the flanks of his horse while digging in his heels, but although the poor horse wanted to gallop; it whinnied humbly, lowered its head, and did not change the rhythm of its trembling steps.

"Let me bear your pain. Don't hurry, apple of my eye, have patience; we're nearly there. You've endured so much, endure a little more. Whatever you do, the horse won't go any faster." With those words Khaja Ibrahim took the edge off the anxiety in the Caravanbashi's soul. Whatever he might do, the only way was to be patient.

As always, the Valley of the Sorcerers opened up suddenly from the colourful depths on the left side of the Invisible

Mountain. Whatever the season, the meadows were green in the home of the sorcerers. This time, the green was a beautiful carpet cast onto the bare earth. Looking up from the mouth of the valley, the riders appreciated the sheer size of the mountain. The triangle was swathed in grey mist. Everything in the world was around that mysterious triangle. The mountain was like a grey curtain hanging from the sky.

No one wanted to climb the Invisible Mountain, because after just a couple of steps the climber seemed to step off the mountainside into thin air. There was a tale of someone who did want to make the ascent. Even if he felt the earth beneath his feet, those watching down below knew that the man's feet were touching nothing; they saw a man ascending to the sky through the air. However, after two or three steps the man lost his courage and, terrified, turned back.

There was just one man, God's slave Husnukaram, of whom the old men of the city whispered that with a dervish's stubbornness he made it to the top of the mountain. Everyone who saw this remembered it. They could not forget as step by step, as though on air, the dervish ascended to the skies. When he reached the top of the mountain, he lay down on the ground to rest a while, opening his arms wide. To the watchers below he looked to have lain down in the emptiness of the sky, or like a bird to have stretched out his wings to fly into the blue. Everyone waited in astonishment. They waited and waited but nothing untoward happened. Dervish Husnukaram returned, again stepping on air as he made his descent, but no one dared approach him when he got back down. No one wanted to talk to the dervish, or even approach him, as he wandered sadly through the city. They were all too wary of him. Husnukaram was also frightened by his adventure and did not want to mix much with people. He soon fell into a sorrowful unease. Everyone passed by on the other side because of his sorrow. Then one day the unexpected happened—he was no longer in the city; he had left and no one saw him again. They said that after Dervish Husnukaram lost his soul he became a sorcerer and lived in the Valley of the Sorcerers. A god-fearing man who went to the valley to bring back a sorcerer claimed to have seen him. But how can anyone truly know?

Chapter 4
Khaja Ibrahim Agha in the Valley of the Sorcerers

The Caravanbashi and Khaja Ibrahim Agha reined in their horses who were about to take fright, steadily stroking them to calm them down. They bent down and whispered something in their ears, but their eyes quickly returned to the road, especially to the right-hand side, as though their gaze deliberately avoided the valley. Their eyes remained on the tail of the caravan winding its way round the Invisible Mountain, though half of it could no longer be seen. It was a trick of the eye, as the head of the caravan had already come down the side of the mountain onto the plain, and soon the caravan would put the Invisible Mountain and the Valley of the Sorcerers behind them.

As the Caravanbashi looked, he sensed but did not see that Ibrahim was no longer with him. He was not surprised. Suddenly, Khaja was not there. This was how it had to be. The solitary path into the Valley of the Sorcerers would take him down to its richly hued central plain where he would find who he was looking for, talk to him, and with him follow the road taken by the Caravanbashi. If everything worked out as they wanted, they would catch up with the caravan as it waited for them on the plain, taking a rest beneath an elm surrounded by bubbling springs in a place known as Gunortaj.

No one had lived there for a long time, but the dismal ruins they had left behind tore at the heart. There were delightful springs and trees and green swards in spring and summer. What the elm alone was worth, why there was no one there, when the last man and woman left, where they went without a backward glance, where they disappeared to, no one knew. The taste of the water in these parts was unique. If anyone from the city passed, they filled their bottles only with water from the springs beneath the elm and took them home. It was at Gunortaj that the Caravanbashi would wait for Ibrahim, stopping the caravan on the pretext of collecting water.

Ibrahim rode quietly down into the valley and stopped at the side of the path. He dismounted and gave the reins to his servant, Nazarali, who was following him. Nazarali tightly tied the bridles of two mules to a bush close to the path, then without uttering a word mounted Ibrahim's horse and galloped towards the tail of the still-hidden caravan without a backward glance.

Ibrahim wrestled a bundle of provisions from the burden carried by one of the mules, hoisted the load onto his shoulder, took one last look towards the distant caravan, straining his eyes searching for Nazarali on the same road, then walked away from the bush along the path. The path wound down into the Valley of the Sorcerers. Calling on the Almighty in his anxious heart and weighed down by the burden on his shoulder, he began to descend the path step by step. He did not know the mystery here, but could hear the beat of his heart. At first he could not see the abundant flora of the valley, but when it opened up before him Ibrahim gazed in silent amazement for a few minutes, though with trepidation in his heart. It was as though all the scents from all four corners of the valley—the grass of the earth, the leaves of the trees, the strong, young intertwined trunks of the shrubs—moved around him, but the imperceptibly moving green life gave him courage and he began to step down into the valley more boldly.

As he descended, he began to spy people. They were all sorcerers. They had already seen him, but the sorcerers weren't at all surprised to see this newcomer. So they already know my purpose, Ibrahim thought. But this wasn't so. The sorcerers didn't know anything yet.

One of them, younger than the others, broke away and came up to Ibrahim, who had already walked a long way down the path into the valley. He was a strapping young sorcerer, with thoughtful eyes and a crooked scar on his cheek. "Salaam Aleykum," the young sorcerer courteously and politely addressed Ibrahim.

Ibrahim was not bold enough to look for long into the young man's sorrowful, pensive face. Turning his astonished gaze aside, he said, "Aleykum salaam."

"I wish you well, respected kinsman. What brings you to these parts?" the young sorcerer asked, again with great courtesy. This time his melancholy voice cut Ibrahim to the quick.

Ibrahim took the bundle full of provisions from his shoulder, set it on the ground, and pushed it under a bush. It was obvious what was in the bundle so no one said a word. But the sorcerers scattered across the valley were curious and slowly began to gather round. They were all very different. It was as though their ordinary appearance, their clothes, their faces, their sheer ordinariness, prompted a deep unease invisible to the naked eye.

Fear of the sorcerers and the valley gripped Ibrahim. He thought that his parched tongue wouldn't be able to say another word if he didn't stammer out now. "Honourable kinsman, I . . .

honourable . . . I am searching for a scholar of the spirit. I want to make contact and pass on a request."

"A scholar of the spirit, you said?" asked a sorcerer, waving his arms in interest, his black beard almost to his waist.

"He said a scholar of the spirit," the young sorcerer who had spied Ibrahim and greeted him so courteously confirmed without turning his head.

"That's not for me then," said the bearded sorcerer and, still waving his arms about, returned to his spot. "He wants to make contact with the spirits," he told two more sorcerers as he passed. Without getting as far as Ibrahim, the two turned back, disappointed. Or at least it seemed to Ibrahim that they were disappointed.

"I know who you need, honoured kinsman. Please, come with me." His eyes as thoughtful as ever, the young sorcerer addressed Ibrahim in a voice brimming with kindness and affection. With the same courtesy, he invited him to follow. "Please, we're going this way."

The young sorcerer in front, Ibrahim set off for the other side of the valley. The sorcerers gathered round and watched them climb the path.

Between rocks, in an area covered with wormwood, where the black earth and its wild vegetation ended, he quietly sat cross-legged, his back towards them. The young sorcerer turned his face towards Ibrahim and said quietly, "This is the person you want." Then he pushed his way in through the vegetation and sat down at his side.

Not knowing what to do, Ibrahim decided to stand a short way away. Whether a long time passed or not, whatever they said and did not say, whether they understood one another or not, it seemed to Ibrahim that the young sorcerer held the other in his sphere of influence. Time passed, and at last both rose to their feet and went to Ibrahim, whose heart was in turmoil.

"This is the person you are looking for," the young sorcerer said with his customary reserve, looking shyly at Ibrahim. "He's ready to go with you, but with certain conditions."

"Please tell me the conditions; I am all ears."

"When he is in the city, he wants no one but you to know that he is there." The young sorcerer nodded towards the man they had come to see.

"Yes, I understand. It will be so, inshallah. But there is one thing—this is not my secret, it's the secret of my master. This is his mission and he is bound to know," Ibrahim said.

The sorcerer and scholar of the spirit was an imposing man, with small eyes and an attentive gaze. His cheeks were smooth; his face had never known bristle or beard. A red cloth was wrapped round his head as a kind of hat. After gazing intently at Ibrahim, he looked over his head towards the Invisible Mountain, as though testing something, mulling something over, and then finally said, "Very well, I agree."

A smile spread across the young man's face and he said to Ibrahim, "Very good, very well. He really is the foremost scholar of the spirit. If he has agreed, then your business will of course go well."

Turning to the imposing sorcerer, he said, "Let not my words fall empty to the ground."

The two sorcerers looked intently at one another, communicating no one knew what in the silence. Then the imposing sorcerer gave a silent nod and set out ahead of them.

The three of them slowly headed for the path going up the valley. Now that he had found the sorcerer he was looking for, Ibrahim thought the other residents of the valley were still watching him but were no longer interested. A sign of courtesy, he thought. They stopped when they reached the path. The young sorcerer bowed lightly towards the other two and placed his hand on his heart.

Ibrahim said, "I thank you for giving your humble servant the honour of witnessing your respect and courtesy."

"Please, there is no need for thanks. It was a great joy and pleasure for me to serve an honoured kinsman such as you," the young sorcerer replied.

When they got to the bottom, they went their separate ways at the bush where the bundle had been left. Turning back once more, the imposing, red-hatted sorcerer led the way. Ibrahim followed him up the path until they eventually reached the caravan road. This time, Ibrahim went ahead, the smooth-cheeked sorcerer behind him. When they reached the mules, the animals were quietly waiting, paying no heed to their surroundings. They untied them and mounted. Ibrahim wanted to look down the valley and catch a final glimpse of the young sorcerer. Sluggishness and unease slipped into his heart.

The two riders, spurring on their mules, were catching up with the caravan. It had passed the same way early that morning, leaving a swirl of dust and smells in its wake.

The sun passed its zenith. Proud and happy as a child that has found what it was looking for, Ibrahim was in seventh heaven. It seemed to him that he was scarcely half an hour in the Valley of the Sorcerers, and if they went a little faster they could catch up with the caravan. But it wasn't so. Ibrahim had, of course, spent a lot longer in the valley than he thought. There was no longer any dust or trace of the caravan.

Lost in their own thoughts, they journeyed in silence.

Ibrahim was not so much talking to himself as quarrelling with himself, setting aside both his earlier alarm and later joy. What if this man dashes our hopes? What a scoundrel I am. Look at me, I took the first person they showed me and set off back. Of course I didn't do the right thing. I should definitely have seen another spirit summoner and chosen between them. That valley is a real bazaar. Why didn't I look?

Sensing the desperate Ibrahim's hidden anxiety, the smooth-cheeked sorcerer said, "I am the only scholar of the spirits that you know in the valley. We all have our own pursuits, but only I make contact with the spirits. You think that you could have found a stronger one. You ask why you took me without looking for another one. Don't worry; whatever you want I will do."

"I don't doubt that, sir . . ."

"My name is Sayyah⁵."

"Sayyah? Is that a nickname or your real name?"

"You want my full name? My full name is Hajji Mir Hasan Agha Sayyah. It's not so cold at the moment, so just call me Sayyah."

"What's the cold got to do with it?"

"When it's cold," Sayyah the Sorcerer grimaced, "I wear this long name like a coat to keep me warm."

Ibrahim was amazed but didn't let it show. "I am Ibrahim Agha. I am in the service of our Padishah's Caravanbashi. I have been at his side for ten years. It's not bad at all."

"The caravan that skirted the Invisible Mountain just before you came—is that yours?"

"Yes, it's ours. We've been on the road for a year now. We've travelled from the Maghreb to the Mashriq. We have visited one hundred cities, seen one hundred bazaars, but have forgotten them all. We're weary, we've no strength left."

---

5 Sayyah (səyyah) means traveller.

"Ibrahim Agha, you'll be home early tomorrow, so why are you grumbling?"

"Me, grumbling? What have I said? I only said that I'm tired." Ibrahim Agha whispered so despondently that his mount could not hear him, but Sayyah the Sorcerer, who was three to four mules behind him heard.

"Don't worry, you'll recover at home. But your tiredness isn't tiredness from the journey, it's something else."

Ibrahim pulled in his neck like a tortoise and held his breath. What's he saying? he wondered.

Sayyah kept on talking, as though to himself, "This tiredness is something else. Even after a long night's rest, you wake up shattered, as though you had been beaten up in your sleep. This is a different tiredness. This is the tiredness of love."

"Sayyah, I am a eunuch. What love are you talking about?" Ibrahim tried to say calmly, forcing himself to keep a straight face.

Sayyah realized that Ibrahim was being generous and wanted to show that he wasn't ashamed of being a eunuch. 'No, that's what I said. So what if you are a eunuch? I can see from your eyes that this tiredness is the tiredness of love." Sayyah suddenly felt very tired himself. "So where will we catch up with the caravan?" he asked, rapidly changing the subject.

"Do you know Gunortaj?"

"I do."

"They'll be waiting for us there."

"We'll get there by evening."

"We're nearly there already."

They carried on in silence. They had already left the Invisible Mountain and Valley of the Sorcerers a long way behind. The greater the distance they put between them, the better Ibrahim felt.

"Sorcerer Sayyah, you never fail when summoning the spirits?" Ibrahim suddenly broke the silence with half a question and half a statement. He took pity on his mount and eased the bridle. Sayyah saw this and did likewise. The mules slowed down. Sayyah rode his mule alongside Ibrahim's.

"The spirits, you said? I have summoned them. What of it?" asked Sayyah.

"Nothing. They came?"

"There were those who came and those who did not."

"You say that some didn't come?"

"They didn't. Isgandar Zulqarney's spirit didn't come. He was stubborn. But a lot did come. Don't you worry, it's only when I'm forced to call them that the spirits don't come. But you haven't forced me, so they will come."

Ibrahim's heart was soothed as though doused by cool water from a mountain waterfall. "If that's how it is, a fine reward is waiting for you, you know," he said.

"Waiting, waiting, you can be sure of that."

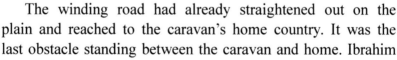

The winding road had already straightened out on the plain and reached to the caravan's home country. It was the last obstacle standing between the caravan and home. Ibrahim breathed in deeply, imprisoning air in his chest. Then slowly he breathed out, releasing the prisoner. Inshallah, everything will turn out fine—it has to turn out fine—and I won't have to hang my head in shame before anyone. Inshallah, this journey will end and his damned father's baleful spirit will come.

Suddenly the Caravanbashi's father, Mammadqulu the Headsman, came unbidden to his mind. A thought flew through Ibrahim's mind. This will be a very hard business, very hard. If the spirit does come, this will be a very hard meeting. When I think of what I have heard of his father, well, the stories may be worse than the truth, or maybe the truth is worse than the stories. He got more pleasure from his profession of headsman than had ever been seen before.

The frosty air of the plain slipped around Ibrahim, caressing his face and eyes, but instead of feeling cold, he felt warm. His consciousness took him away somewhere, but then he straightened up and remembered that he was riding a mule. All his pains left him one by one and Ibrahim dozed off as he rode.

CHAPTER 5
The Shah and His Favourite Headsman

He served his beloved Shah with great zeal. It was enough for the word headsman to slip from the Shah's lips to carry to the other side of the rich red curtain hanging behind the enormous throne, on which the Shah took up just one corner, for Mammadqulu to appear at his protector's side, bowing as low to the ground as possible. First he would look for the Shah himself in that vast throne, and when he found him would look for his face and eyes, and when he saw those large, sparkling luminous eyes, the Pivot of the Universe would not need to say another word, as his eyes would say everything. Mammadqulu the Headsman had never misread what was written in those eyes.

Every type of punishment had its own look on the Shah's face. If a head had to be chopped off, the pupils of the Shah's eyes seemed to shiver with cold and gaze in revulsion. If an eye had to be gouged out, his eyelids closed as though it were night. Darkness covered the light of the eyes of the Pivot of the Universe and this light's final act was to reveal to Mammadqulu the mystery of this punishment. If an ear had to be cut off, the ears of the Pivot of the Universe twitched. If someone had to be broken, he shot across his throne in a strange, dance-like

27

movement, and his eyes looked narrow and sour.

The idea had never once come to the Pivot of the Universe of telling Mammadqulu in words the type of punishment. The mystery of the punishment passed from eye to eye, from glance to glance. No sooner had it passed than, with a single hand, the pitiless headsman would slit the throat of a poor wretch, wrench his feet from the ground, raise him up, tuck him under his arm, and before he lost consciousness, take one final look at the Pivot of the Universe to see if his intention had changed in those few seconds, if he wanted to impose a different punishment, or pardon the culprit of his sins.

This had only happened once in all those long and at the same time short years. After summoning Mammadqulu, who was throttling a poor old wretch as he picked him up, only once did the Pivot of the Universe give the sign to stop and then say, "You can go."

A few moments earlier such a spark had flashed in the depths of the Pivot of the Universe's shivering eyes, or maybe it had been the glimmer of a tear. Mammadqulu, who already had the victim by the throat with one hand, set the weak, near unconscious old man down on his trembling legs, bowed low, touched the ground with his forehead and did not know what to do next, feeling he had been interrupted. This was the first time that he did not know what to do. The headsman, who had spent his life in the palace in the shadow of the shah, had until this time sensed with the hair of his body every movement, every glance of the Shah, and for the first time did not know whether to leave his presence or remain.

"Leave him for now, Mammadqulu. Go and wait outside. Let him go. Let this . . . cruel old man go," the pensive Shah said. Then he turned such a hard gaze upon him that Mammadqulu clasped his hands to his beating heart and afterwards could not say how he left the royal presence.

The Pivot of the Universe stared thoughtfully at the old man. Then he gave a sign with his hand and the guards picked him up from the floor, straightened him up, and stood on either side to make sure he didn't collapse again. The Shah said, "Old man, I will ask you one more time. I am told that you killed your son and then took his wife for you own. Is this true?"

His head hanging down and without the strength to move it, the old man stammered, "It is true, Pivot . . . of the Universe."

With sudden clarity the Shah said, "No, it is not true. A thought has just come to me. What village did you say you are from?"

The old man summoned the last of his strength to say, "I am from Sellama." His head remained on his chest.

The Shah nodded in agreement. "So you are from Sellama. It's all clear now. This is the truth. This is the doing of your village elder. You've been told to take the blame yourself, and if you don't . . ."

With great effort, the old man raised his mournful head and gazed pleadingly at the Shah. The Shah continued, "If you don't, he will kill your grandsons. You have got grandsons, haven't you, old man? Yes, of course you have. If you don't admit guilt, he threatened to kill your grandsons, didn't he? What's his name, this village elder? It isn't Bayramali, is it?"

"I killed him, Pivot of the Universe, I did. Yes, his name's Bayramali. I'm miserable, I'm wretched, I'm poor, and I'm bad." The old man sobbed, tears pouring down his face into his beard.

The Shah cheered up. Solving the crime had given him a lightness of heart. Why am I wasting my time with this old man? he thought to himself. Turning to his chief servant, he gave him an order. "Bring that son of a cur, Bayramali, here and quickly. Tie him to the horse's tail, knock him to the ground, beat him

until . . . beat him, but be sure not to kill him. This old man
will kill him. He must avenge his son. Vengeance must not be
forgotten! Why am I on this throne? Don't be afraid, old man,
get your breath back."

The Shah turned to face the old man and nodded to the
guards. They carefully took him aside and set him down on a
cushion. The old man was barely conscious, but tears continued
to trickle from his closed eyes into his beard.

In due course, Bayramali was dragged to the palace and
thrown like a sack of dung at the foot of the throne. The Shah
raged, "Get him up!"

They raised Bayramali to his knees. His fury unabated, the
Shah yelled, "Bayramali, you son of a cur, look at this old man.
Do you know him?"

With difficulty, Bayramali raised his wretched head. As soon
as he saw the old man, he understood and his eyes lost their light.

This time the Shah spoke with a false friendliness.
"Bayramali, do you know why I came to suspect you?" Then he
answered his own question, "Because this is already the second
such event in this village. Do you remember the old man two
years ago, goddamn you? He was so vilified that I had him killed.
Now I know that the wretch was not guilty. Son of a cur, why is
it that fathers have started killing their sons and seducing their
daughters-in-law only in your village? Have you all suddenly
lost your heads?"

Baryamali the village elder saw that it was over and that the
Shah knew everything. Without saying another word, he began
to bang his head against the floor.

"Didn't you have a mother and father, son of a cur?" the enraged Shah asked, shouting so loudly at that Mammadqulu rushed in and stood behind Bayramali like winged Azrael, the Angel of Death, and awaited orders.

Bayramali gave no answer but continued to bang his head against the floor. His head should have long since burst like a watermelon, but it swelled up instead.

"Take this wretch away." The Shah looked with loathing at Bayramali, and finally turned to Mammadqulu, the pupils of his eyes flickering, shivering. "But make sure that this old man himself . . ." Without another word, the Shah rose and left the throne room.

Mammadqulu grabbed Bayramali so tightly by the throat that he could only wheeze and then dragged him outside. Two guards, accompanied by Vizier Mashdali, took the poor old man by the arms and wanted to lift him to his feet. The old man had already come around. He pushed away their hands and stood up resolutely. Without waiting for their help, he walked steadily out of the room.

When Mammadqulu saw that the village elder did not want to leave and was dragging his feet, he began to talk sweetly to the wretch, as to a sheep about to be slaughtered. "Come, servant of God, stand up, don't drag your feet. Thank the Pivot of the Universe for not wiping out your whole family. You have one soul and today or tomorrow it will leave your body; it will fly away. Come, don't be afraid."

Speaking these words, he took the elder to the place of execution in the courthouse yard. He told the helpers who were waiting for him, "Hurry up and tie this one's legs. Oh dear, look at him. God's creature, be quiet! Don't try my patience. He's kicking. Stop kicking, son of a donkey. I said stop kicking!"

He moved aside, took a large knife, and thrust it into the

hands of the old man, who was trembling with rage, his eyes ablaze. "You begin," he said.

In the iron grip of the headsman's assistants, the elder fell still and silent, simply jerking his head from time to time. First the old man, and then Mammadqulu, slowly, taking pleasure, slit the man's throat, as though chopping off a chicken's head. Mammadqulu's moustache was bright red from the gushing blood.

Wasn't the magnificently moustachioed Mammadqulu the Pivot of the Universe's favourite headsman? Of course he was.

CHAPTER 6

The Caravanbashi's Secret

Whe Ibrahim reached the road to the plain he truly felt he had grown wings and could fly. He had already begun to trust Sayyah. They had found a common language and his heart was at peace. He was confident that the Caravanbashi's dream would come true, the matter would be re-solved, and they would both at last find solace. His heart, which had long been constrained, finally opened up on the plain. He flew like a bird. He noticed how many times he felt complete peace in his soul, his spirit, after reaching the plain's road, and as he drowsed on horseback he felt himself soaring through the seventh heaven like a falcon.

The plain road could be said to be home. It was also busy, and you always met fellow travellers along the way. The plain road had two carriageways. There were stretches where people are always coming from one direction or another, and there are parts where you won't meet another living soul either by daylight or moonlight.

While travelling on the road Ibrahim was suddenly struck by a thought. It was on this road that he seemed to be travelling on the body of an enormous woman. Her body was covered in moles, warts, and boils, large and small. The main city of the land was a mole, maybe a boil—no, not a boil, a mole. Now the caravan was moving at a camel's pace, while he was far behind, moving at a mule's pace, but with every step they were coming closer. With every step the mole was getting bigger, and at the same time every flaw in this enormous body was becoming less visible. Slowly, the mole turned into the city.

They rode their mules, sometimes in silence, sometimes with two or three words flying between them, until at last from afar they spied the enormous, near-frozen trunk of the elm rising up in the middle of Gunortaj, and darkness slowly began to fall.

Nazarali the camel boy was the first to spot Ibrahim and Sayyah. "I'll get my reward," he said and hurried into the tent.

"Master, they have come! There are two people, Ibrahim Agha and someone very tall."

Murmuring "Thank you, Almighty," the Caravanbashi gave the boy the promised two silver coins. Hiding the excitement in his heart, he said with studied nonchalance to the joyful Nazarali, "Give them food and drink, then send them to me."

The caravan would spend the night here. It would be the last night before reaching home. The people of the caravan were all busy washing and cleaning, not resting. Some fetched water from the spring, heated it over the campfire, and then scrubbed away the dirt from the past year from head to toe. Others mended holes in clothes and socks, while others put their garments to rights.

The return of the caravan was, of course, a cause for celebration for the city. Sarvan the camel driver had already sent a herald to the city. Pipers and drummers would welcome them.

All the people of the city would turn out to watch the spectacle. The camels' bells, the colourful bridles, reins, and packsaddles of the horses and mules, the strange garments of the servants and camel drivers, the like of which had not been seen in these parts for a thousand years—a spectacle, without doubt a spectacle.

When Sayyah and Ibrahim entered the tent, the Caravanbashi was sitting cross-legged on a small carpet in the far corner, a carefree expression playing on his face. With one elbow on a bolster, he slowly turned large amber prayer beads with the fleshy fingers of his other hand, murmuring a chant. After looking Sayyah over from top to toe, he motioned them both to sit down.

"Welcome," the Caravanbashi said in greeting. In turn they greeted him courteously and went to sit opposite him. Sayyah and the Caravanbashi were facing each other, while Ibrahim sat cross-legged near the Caravanbashi's bolster, practically beneath his hand.

"Who is this gentleman with you and why has he come?" Again banishing his anxiety, the Caravanbashi spoke as calmly as he could, because he had heard that this was how you should put the first question. Let's see how much he knows. If I let him into my secret, I might be sorry later, the Caravanbashi thought to himself.

Ibrahim immediately understood the Caravanbashi's intent and joined the game. Glancing at Sayyah, he said, "Master, may I introduce the famous scholar, Haji Mir Hasan Agha Sayyah. His name is well known to scholars of the spirits and to the whole community of scientists. We became acquainted in the Valley of the Sorcerers.

"When the caravan was rounding the Invisible Mountain, I had the idea to go down into the valley, as I had business there. I did not want to trouble you and knew that I would catch up to you at Gunortaj. When I saw Sayyah Agha, I thought that I should acquaint this scholar with you. I apprised him of my intent. He gave his consent, as I had already told him of your interest in the science of the spirits. I am grateful that he did not disappoint me and came. Master, this is our guest. Sayyah, this is our master whom I told you about, the solution to all our troubles."

The Caravanbashi just managed to rouse himself to interrupt Ibrahim. "Very good, very good. That's enough. He is our guest and is welcome. Has the guest been offered food and drink, Khaja Ibrahim?"

"Yes, my lord, he has. Don't worry about anything."

"To your good health, we have eaten and drunk very well," Sayyah said, expressing his heartfelt thanks.

"Bring some tea. Would you like sherbet?"

"Why not, master? Yes, we'll drink some sherbet," Ibrahim said.

"Help yourself, please, Haji Agha!" The Caravanbashi turned towards Sayyah. "I can see you've reached quite an age. You must be over fifty, but probably haven't lived all your life in that valley. What corner of this land are you from? Where have you been? Where have the winds carried you? Where did you study? Who was your teacher? What fate took you to that valley of miracles?

"Night is slowly falling and will slowly pass. It's a winter night and we're in no hurry to go anywhere. Our heart will be cheered if you talk to us. Of course, if what I asked is a secret . . ."

Of course, it's important to put me through this kind of test, Sayyah thought. So he slowly turned towards the Caravanbashi and replied, "What is a secret will remain a secret, but what is not a secret will be made known. A secret that has been stripped bare and naked is no longer a secret."

The Caravanbashi fixed his gaze on a solitary, large black fly which had managed to get in somehow and was buzzing loudly around the tent. Then he turned away from the fly and looked at Sayyah, beginning to listen to what he was saying with even more interest.

Sayyah took a breath and slowly continued. "I am from a very faraway place, Master. I don't believe that you and your caravan have ever been to those parts, or that you ever will. Our people call the land the Wheel of Fate. They conduct their lives, their faith, their conversations, and relations like a wheel of fate, a circle. Everything is round. Their way of walking and their way of life resembles a circle. To them, not only their homes but the whole world, the whole universe, is a circle, an orb, a wheel. My compatriots never travel a straight road; they always plot a circular route. They build their houses round; they cannot accept straight lines or corners. When an arrow is shot, it is certain to return to the archer after it has hit its target, because the Great Circle has its own attraction. If the arrow does not return, this means it has found a hole in the void enveloping this world and flown into another world.

"Whatever is written must, without fail, yearn for its beginning like a circle. The meaning of our written works, if read from end to beginning, is the same as from beginning to end. After leaving the land of the Wheel of Fate it is impossible to go to any other country. Whoever has tried to do this has failed. They have walked around and around and returned to their starting point. Since ancient times it has been the destiny of only one man to leave the Wheel of Fate and journey to another land. That person stands before you, honoured sir."

After he had finished speaking, Sayyah took a pitcher of sherbet from a low table in front of him, poured some into his bowl. He took the bowl in his hand but did not drink, as though he wanted to warm the contents, and then continued to speak in the same slow, measured tone.

"Yes, you may be surprised and you may not believe me, but I have told you the truth. I am the only person, the only citizen of the land of the Wheel of Fate, who has found a new, very different homeland far away beneath the Invisible Mountain. But of course I did not reach that land straightaway. I journeyed through many lands and saw many cities. Do not ask how I was able to escape the gravity of the Great Circle and end up here—that is quite a different subject, one of the greatest secrets, which can be of no interest to you."

The Caravanbashi and Ibrahim listened to Sayyah with ever-growing interest and enthusiasm. As soon as Sayyah paused for breath, the Caravanbashi exchanged glances with Ibrahim and tried to steer the conversation towards the subject that was troubling him.

"But where did you learn this science of the spirit, Haji Agha?" the Caravanbashi asked. "Was it in your homeland or somewhere else?"

"In another time and another place, my teacher learned the science of the spirit from Manuchohr ibn Sadiq. Of course, you must have heard of him, yes? Yes, he learned from Manuchohr ibn Sadiq himself."

"Manuchohr ibn Sadiq, you said?" Nonplussed, the Caravanbashi twitched in his seat.

Ibrahim appeared bewitched, his eyes half closed. Words suddenly spilled from his lips by rote, a rich, melancholy sound in the silence. "Those who are not yet born into this world but will be born have spirits too. The spirits of those not yet born roam around us, trying to make contact with the spirits of those already born into this world . . ."

At that point, Sayyah took up the words of Khaja Ibrahim with deep respect, speaking in the same rich, melancholy voice. ". . . with a child's enthusiasm and a child's stubbornness they want to learn from them about the world, about the lands here, about life. The spirits of the dead, sometimes patient and restrained, sometimes impatient, tell them what they know and what they do not know, of what they have heard and of what they have not heard. They look with sadness and bitterness at these impatient spirits who listen to their words with great respect and desire, with unbounded interest and fervour, who long to learn from them and await their turn to come into this world."

Sayyah stopped speaking and smiled at Ibrahim, who repeated the last sentence. "When they come into this world, they forget whatever was on that side, whatever happened there." He then spoke from the heart, "Of course, Manuchohr ibn Sadiq was a very great scholar. May God grant the teacher peace."

The Caravanbashi pondered a while. What he had heard seemed almost like blasphemy to him. Come what may, our religion does not yet ban the study of the spirits, or if it does, I know nothing of it, he thought, trying to calm himself, and then returned to the conversation with the visitor.

"Your words are like gold. This man really was your teacher's teacher?"

"Yes, he was. I heard much praise of this great person from my teacher and remember his words."

"Your teacher . . . ?" Ibrahim did not say the name that had come to him in a flash. He kept silent, cutting short his own words, because he did not want to say the name, but to ask a tired question to which he already knew the answer.

"My teacher, Ibrahim Agha, is al-Zatiney the White, the Dervish from the Islands. I expect you know this name well." Sayyah again read what was on Ibrahim's mind.

"The very same?" Ibrahim's eyes flashed like those of a lone, hungry wolf fixed on its prey.

I foretold this. The White Dervish was a wanderer, far

removed from religion and faith. I knew all this did not concern
our religion, thought the downcast Caravanbashi.

"It does not harm religion."

This time, sensing what was in the Caravanbashi's heart,
Sayyah responded, "My teacher worked for a long time to
prove this to the ulema[6] in Damascus, Aleppo, and Hajeb. He
succeeded with some, but not with others. Disappointed, he
headed for the mountains and built himself a hut where he lived
as an ascetic. He accepted only those pupils whom he trusted,
passing on his limitless knowledge to them and deepening the
science of the spirits."

"Yes, yes, of course we heard of this."

"Your teacher was the White Dervish." Ibrahim's eyes
brimmed with hidden delight.

Of course, he knew that the White Dervish had not gone
to the mountains of his own will. The last time the influential
ulema of the Great Clerical Council had met in Aleppo it had
been to discuss the foundations of the science of the spirits and
religion. The discussions slowly turned into a trial. For nine days
they exposed the White Dervish as a knave who had gone astray,
in whose soul jinns and genies and mad spirits had settled, who
had strayed from God's path, an enemy of religion, who spoke
in the name of the heavens and spirits, but had no right to do so.

The White Dervish's constant rival, a very influential member
of the Great Clerical Council, The Yellow Sayid Asrar, also
known as the Yellow Sayid[7], was the one who had craftily turned
the discussion into a trial. On the last day of the discussions,
just before the verdict was decided, the White Dervish could
bear it no longer. He told the Yellow Sayid exactly what he

---

6 A body of Muslim scholars with special knowledge of Islamic law.
7 Sayid is an honorary title for a Muslim who can trace his descent from the
Prophet Muhammad.

thought of him, and also heaped abuse on other members of the clerical council. Recklessly, he even humiliated the religious figures who were serving as judges. Then he left the discomfited council of his own accord, and for a long time no one knew his whereabouts.

Eventually, one of his pupils who had left the Red Mountain near Hajeb to go to the city to buy provisions was followed by secret agents. They found where the White Dervish was living and reported it to religious officials. Some say that this pupil was a spy for the agents, others that he was linked to the Yellow Sayid. Deliberately or not, this person betrayed the White Dervish. But there were also those who maintained that the pupil was innocent from start to finish.

In a nutshell, after discovering where the White Dervish was living, the secret agents bound him hand and foot in chains and brought him to the court of the ulema of the Great Clerical Council, guardians of the purity of their religion. A death sentence was pronounced. At midnight the same day, before the death sentence was carried out, he was beaten in the square outside the courthouse. Without further ado, a senior executioner crucified the desiccated dervish, and then chopped his grey-bearded head from his old, inert body.

This time a rumour spread in the city that his faithful disciples had taken an oath to avenge his death. The rumour said that the disciples would commit suicide to close the paths of communication between mankind and the spirits, which he had searched for and taught them how to find, once and for all.

After their departure from this life, no one would remain in their place because they were the last on the road to making contact with the spirits. No one else would ever devote themselves to the White Dervish, and no one would ever know the secret. It is said that when the time for suicide came, twenty-three young disciples, who called themselves the White Dervish's Shadows, banished one person, or sent him away, and did not afford him the honour of committing suicide with them. When twenty-three white-clad figures jumped hand-in-hand from the mountaintop into the black abyss, looking for all the world like a flock of cranes, one onlooker stood on the opposite cliff, an offended smile playing on his sour face as he gazed into infinity above their heads. Ibrahim felt his blood freeze in his veins as another thought flashed through his mind. He couldn't take his eyes off Sayyah the Sorcerer's face.

Lost in his own mind, the Caravanbashi was unaware of the thoughts passing through Ibrahim's head. The secret, silent conversation between Sayyah and Ibrahim did not concern him. His thoughts fixed on just the one, well-known subject. Yes, there was no doubt. The sorcerer was a sorcerer. He looked like a sorcerer, and if you studied him carefully you could see that he was a man in the midst of mystery.

This time, wanting to show just a little of what interested him, the Caravanbashi said carefully, "God willing, we shall be home tomorrow. We shall rest, and tomorrow evening or the next day, whichever is better, Ibrahim Agha will tell you of our work. What do you say to that?"

The question of course was addressed only to Sayyah, who replied, "Master, as you wish. Tomorrow or the day after—what difference does it make? Only, I want the sky to be the right colour." As though muttering to himself, he continued, "As long as the sky is the colour that I need, it doesn't matter what's on earth."

The conversation finished there, like a snack that failed to satisfy the stomach. In the middle of the night, the Caravanbashi slipped into his warm bed. For a long time he was occupied with his thoughts. Then, tossing and turning his weak body, he eventually fell into a sleep, the like of which he had not experienced for many years. He sobbed as his languorous, green-eyed mother came to him in his dream.

CHAPTER 7
Beautiful parnisa and Headsman Mammadqulu

One day in this small, vainglorious city, Mammadqulu had his first glimpse of the young widow who was to befuddle his brain and muddle his thoughts. She lived with her old grandmother in one of the crooked streets in the upper quarter of the city. The city had not been able to withstand the Shah's forces for more than two days and it shamefully had to beg for mercy, though no one could say why it had revolted in the first place. The widow's husband departed this world in that two-day, mismatched fight.

The single window on the second floor of the house on the crooked street, where Mammadqulu had made his home after driving out the owners, looked directly over the young widow's courtyard. By God, how much light that window let in in the early hours of the morning! The window opened like the eye of a crane onto the small yard of the beautiful Parnisa's house.

Since the magnificently moustachioed executioner could not tear himself away from this window, he gradually attracted the attention of the neighbours. Even without this, the headsman who had defeated an army was an endless topic of conversation, not just in his own neighbourhood, but throughout the city.

44

"He came."

"No."

"You saw it as well as I did."

"He's got so many swords in his house, so many axes . . ."

"Well, he is a headsman."

"Look carefully into his eyes and you won't see an ounce of pity."

"His face could be a thousand-year-old glacier."

"He can't take his eyes off the lovely Parnisa's courtyard."

"Is he stuck to that window, or what?"

"Are his sort allowed to take a wife?"

"Yes."

"No."

"Why not?"

"Didn't you see that day . . ."

This was the kind of tittle-tattle that had already begun to walk, limp, and stagger through the crooked streets.

Mammadqulu did not know why he had been so impatient lately, where he was always hurrying to. Though he really did know where he was hurrying to—to the bird's eye window. Soon after the sun set, the little girl would bolt the door and not stick her nose outside again. Mammadqulu would not be able to see her again that day and would impatiently tug his horse's bridle. His heart would clench and he would begin to kick harder and harder against his horse's flanks.

It must have been on the third day after he moved into that house that he went up to the room's only big window and, while he lazily contemplated the sparkling dome of the Friday mosque, suddenly felt a gaze from the neighbour's yard boring into his unshaven face like the tip of a burning spear. She was rather short and thin, but a real black beauty. She carried a wooden bowl full of washed, wrung-out clothes and was about to hang them on the line that ran from one corner of the roof to the tip of the fence in the small yard when she shook her hair back, raised her head, and saw a swarthy, bushy moustachioed man at the neighbours' window, gazing thoughtfully at the mosque. Entranced, she stared at that sad face and couldn't stop herself saying, "God help us, do they too have their God? Do headsmen too know mercy?"

A bride for just one year, it had been less than a month since the beautiful Parnisa had lost her young husband. He had been one of the defenders of the town. He had rushed off that evening as if to meet his end. The young bride, who had always had a smile on her lips, was changed completely by his martyrdom. She had had her fill of crying, but the smile had left her face, flown away somewhere else.

"Where on earth are you, Parnisa? How long does it take to hang out some washing?"

Parnisa started like a gazelle that scents a wild animal as she heard the old woman's voice, croaky as a hag's, coming from the house. She wiped her moist green eyes with the back of her hand, or maybe she raised her hand to tear her gaze away from the window, and then began quickly to take the clothes from the bowl and hang them out on the line. The old grandmother's voice brought Mammadqulu back to earth too, and for the first time from his window on the second floor he saw the small, straight-haired beauty in the small yard.

He studied the girl. His first thought was, "What a delicate neck she has; that would take only one strike."

He swatted this thought like a fly out of his mind. He directed his gaze towards the girl once more. He watched her for some time. He enjoyed watching her like this. He comfortably contemplated her figure, her posture, and her supple body as she hung out the washing, murmuring something to herself. She saw me watching, but thought nothing of it.

Down below, the lovely Parnisa suddenly realised that every move she made, every time she stooped and stood up, every time she twisted her body like a fish, she was doing it to spite the older, moustachioed man who was so brazenly watching her. Or maybe she wasn't spiting him. As this thought occurred to her, her face flushed a deep, dawn red. She suddenly turned her head and fixed her brazen gaze on the hawkish eyes of this man. Her gaze caught his. They got tangled up and then fell slack; neither could stop staring sorrowfully at the other.

"Everyone is afraid of you, I know, but I am not so afraid. I am not at all afraid."

"Why should you be afraid of me? I don't know you and you don't know me. Don't be afraid."

"I'm not afraid. I'm never afraid."

"It's good not to be afraid. I am no cannibal."

"You are a cannibal. Don't try to deceive me. You chop off heads. How many guilty and innocent people have perished at your hand?"

"No, don't say that. Everyone has their own guilt. The innocent are the guilty whose guilt cannot be seen."

"Why are you talking standing up there? Can't you see I've got work to do? Don't look at me like that. Granny is coming now."

The old woman slowly waddled up, angrily took the washing from the lovely Parnisa, pushed her aside, and struggled to hang out the clothes herself. This time she opened her mouth like a bent old witch but made no sound.

Day slowly followed day, but the hours and the minutes passed like lightning. Slowly drying her eyes, from that day forward the lovely Parnisa saw the same moustache stuck onto the fleshy face at the upstairs window next door whenever she went out into the backyard,. She knew that the sharp gaze of the owner of the moustache waited for her and followed her every move. She would have sworn that his gaze was very sad, that this was a sad man, not a brazen one.

He really did try to hide from Parnisa; sometimes he succeeded and sometimes he did not. When he did not succeed, it was as though his sorrowful looks called out to her, attracted the beautiful Parnisa like a magnet, leading her along a flower-strewn path. His gaze said to her, "Come, girl. I, who all my life have never known true love, true delight, longing, or togetherness, have never known for what and for whom to sacrifice my life."

If anyone watched from the side during those moments they would never have thought that this was the gaze of Mammadqulu the Headsman. Something, or someone else, was looking out through Mammadqulu's eyes; another type of man looked this way. Even her husband of less than a year had never looked at her in such a way. Parnisa's heart trembled as though in a sweet dream. She hoped never to wake without him, and in this dream did whatever he wanted her to do. She was quite brazen! She took a ladder, propped it against the wall, climbed up to that window on the second floor, scrambled inside, took that bushy moustache, stretched it, and plunge herself into the embrace of those mighty arms.

When moonlight flooded the yard and grandma's snoring rocked the house, what did Parnisa see? She saw herself climbing the ladder rung by rung along the flower-strewn path up to the second floor. How her heart thudded. When Mammadqulu reached down and took her by the waist, he did not know what time he lifted her like a bird through the window, or what time he placed her in the middle of the room.

Poor thing, there there now, I need to calm down too. Whatever will be will be.

Let it be later.

No, now not later.

No, it's impossible now, another time.

No, now.

Oh, God, if she finds out, Grandma will kill me.

I'll be your sacrifice, let me go.

What am I doing here anyway?

Oh God, I am your sacrifice, believe me.

Let me go, I'll come back tomorrow. She'll go to the village; tomorrow is good. Let me go, for God's sake let me go! If she finds out, she will punish me severely. I am unlucky, wretched, and pitiful.

Shush, don't say anything.

Why though? Why me in this big city? You could have whoever you wanted. Stop, stop! Be patient, you have no patience. Why have you no patience? Oh, God, oh God, why does he have no patience—none! You're not fair, not fair. Your . . . look at that brazen moustache, just look, rocking, rocking . . .

Parnisa and Mammadqulu wrapped themselves around each other, and the whispers that could not separate them slowly began to melt in the dark, heavy silence. As soon as she said "let me go," a wisp of clouds covered the moon, smothering the yard in darkness. When that cloud would move away from the moon, God alone knew.

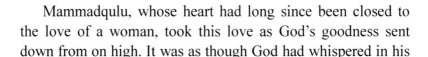

Mammadqulu, whose heart had long since been closed to the love of a woman, took this love as God's goodness sent down from on high. It was as though God had whispered in his

ear, "Can you see that girl? Take her, save her from sorrow and
misfortune, never let her go."

Unable to forget that whisper, Mammadqulu hugged Parnisa
so close to his hairy chest that the girl cried out in fright, "I can't
breathe! Let me go, let me go, you're killing me! My God, what
are you doing? Are you mad? You're mad, for God's sake, mad."
He loved to hear her say this, but he was not really enjoying
what she said, but the sound of her voice.

It was also strange that recently Mammadqulu had begun to
talk sweetly in a voice from the heart. Everyone was astounded.
They said this wasn't the furious, formidable Mammadqulu; it
was a different man. He was a different person at work too. He
saw the beautiful Parnisa wherever he looked. He had clearly
cooled towards his work. He had to force himself to get some
work done every day. He tried not to tempt fate, to get through
the day so that he could go home.

When he was home he waited for the moonlight. When
moonlight flooded the yard, Parnisa placed the ladder against
the wall and knocked at the bird's eye window without a hint of
shame. Mammadqulu's heart was like a string stretched taut and
at that moment it would snap. As the girl climbed the ladder, he
paced the room from side to side, nearly moving to the next world
in his agitation. When he knew that she was coming waiting was
not so bad, but his whole being found a sweet pleasure, like
honey, in this waiting. If anyone had told him before that he
would so long for someone that waiting would be sweet and he
would forget everything else, Mammadqulu would have laughed
in his face.

"When the Shah leaves will you go with him?"

"I am a servant, God's humble slave. Who am I? I cannot
but go."

"You mean you'll go?"

"Of course I'll go."

"And what about me?"

"What about you?"

"Me. You said you loved me!"

"I did?"

"Yes."

"Then I love you."

"No, now I know you don't love me. You don't love me in the slightest."

Parnisa could continue her he-loves-me, he-loves-me-not conversation for hours, half asleep, until the first light of morning came, but he took no offence. Mammadqulu's fingers dreamily wandered through her ruffled hair. He held her close, as though he was hugging her soul, just as he had hugged his mother's warm belly as a child. This pleasure was rather different. The beautiful Parnisa was a copy of his mother. Her voice was the same too.

"So let those who are going go, but not you. I won't let you go, you know. I need a husband, no one else. You cannot abandon me. You cannot get away from me. I'm right, Mammadqulu."

But instead of Mammadqulu, he heard Zabulla Agha. The words were all the same. His mother had said those words to one-legged Zabulla. Less than a month after his father's death, she had made the bed out in his yard under the cool mulberry tree—no, under the elm tree—and his mother and one-legged Zabulla had lain down together, their bodies entwined. So those very same words were imprinted on his memory. His mother had said the same things, and for him the lovely Parnisa was now the same as his mother.

CHAPTER 8

The Sorcerers of the Valley

T he nightingales sang in the lush green of the Valley of the Sorcerers in spring. The young sorcerer sat in his usual spot, leaning one shoulder against a nearly bare rock that seemed to grow out of the earth, but this time he looked out of the valley up towards the Invisible Mountain, gazing thoughtfully in its direction. Of course, the mountain remained invisible as usual, but snow had fallen all night, covering the mountain and turning it into a giant snowball. The wind whipped the white snow in all directions. Where the valley ended and the lower slopes of the Invisible Mountain began, the strong wind was doing its work, causing a blizzard. The snow fell silently, covering the area in pure white.

Down below in the valley everything was, as always, quite different. The chirping of the birds and babbling of the brooks slipped from the air into the ground, from the ground into every particle of the air. The sounds slipped right inside the rich colours. No, the sounds didn't slip into the many colours, the sounds slipped out of them.

In twos and threes the sorcerers strolled from one side of the valley to the other, deep in conversation, without a thought for the world beyond, some of them arguing and waving their arms around, some talking quietly, others in great agitation. The

52

world beyond the valley was of no importance to them. Here in this valley they were like fish in the sea. Now and then the others glanced in the young sorcerer's direction to check that he was in his usual spot and then sighed with relief. The young sorcerer, however, sat motionless, gazing sorrowfully towards the Invisible Mountain. It was as though he was looking for something inside the blizzard. He was looking and looking but could not find it. He had a presentiment that something very important was about to happen nearby. But what? He knew but at the same time did not know.

CHAPTER 9

Home

A hidden pride lay in the Caravanbashi's eyes as he looked the caravan over from beginning to end. He rode up to a high spot from where the caravan opened up like a richly coloured carpet across the plain. Despite the hue and cry and the weight of its burdens, with hidden fervour the caravan was taking the last enthusiastic steps on its long journey. He gave his horse its head and re-joined the caravan, riding alongside Ibrahim and Sayyah, who had swapped their mules for horses.

"Ibrahim Agha, take Haji Agha to our house, put him in the upper guest room, and make sure he is well looked after," the Caravanbashi said.

"Yes, Master, don't worry. I will do whatever is needed."

"I shall have a great many things to do. We have to go to the caravansary and unload the caravan. And before that, of course I must go into the presence of the Pivot of the Universe. God willing, we shall meet at home this evening."

Sayyah felt in his heart that he should say something, as he had held his tongue all the way. "Whatever you wish, we will do. Rest assured you will get what you want from me. What happens afterwards is not my concern."

He immediately regretted his last words. I shouldn't have gone that far, he thought. But he knew from experience how many people spared no effort in summoning the spirits of their loved ones and poured money into it. But how did it end? In sorrow and sadness.

The Caravanbashi did not show his displeasure at the last remark. Discomfited, Ibrahim shook his head and turned to look at Sayyah. An awkward silence followed. They rode on for some time without speaking. They were already passing the first houses and hamlets. Although they had not quite reached the real frosts of winter, traces of the first snow that had fallen a few days before lay beneath the bushes in the yards, on the tree tops, and the roofs of the houses. The eyes, tired of seeing green for so long, seemed to rest as they gazed at this whiteness. The frosty air that had whipped up a blizzard around the Invisible Mountain would reach the rear of the caravan in a few days' time. But would there be the strength and patience for the snow piled up in the nooks and crannies?

Ibrahim's breath hung in the air. I'll break this awkward silence, he thought and turned to Sayyah the Sorcerer. "Master Sayyah, the climate makes your valley a piece of paradise, praise God. How is it that the different seasons pass on all sides of your valley but do not enter your gorge, which always enjoys a fine spring? Is this the result of your actions or is there another secret?"

"What do you think, Haji Agha? How can it be winter all around, with nature complaining bitterly and blizzards everywhere—the Invisible Mountain is blanketed with snow right now—how can there be lush foliage, flowers, springs, and birds singing in the trees when there is frost everywhere else?"

"Of course, Sayyah Agha, I imagine that there is another mystery. Of course, it is the result of your powers. You have brought paradise to this world, praise God."

"Now that I am here with you, a small hole has opened

up in the valley's surface. If my friends do not close it, the snowstorm will pass through this hole into the valley," Sayyah said thoughtfully.

The city was a large black dot slowly coming towards them. As it grew, the occasional houses turned into narrow streets, then the narrow streets grew wider, then trees, water channels, and fountains appeared. All along the road people came out to welcome the caravan. But this was not yet the city itself. The gates to the city were still ahead of them. The caravan was not moving as quickly as before. It had slowed its pace, intoxicated with the interest and good will directed its way. Now that the gates to the city could be glimpsed from afar, horses galloped up to the caravan. The Caravanbashi rode to the head of the caravan where Qotazli was taking languid, stately steps.

"Congratulations, Master, we have reached home," Qarasuvarli the camel driver said as he rode up to him.

"Congratulations to you too, Qara. Congratulations to all of us," the Caravanbashi replied. "Have the dogs been muzzled?"

"They have, and they're also tied up with chains. Don't worry."

The sound of the pipes and drums grew louder. The camels stopped for a moment to eat hay, then moved forward again, following the camel drivers and chewing hay.

Cheered by the welcome, the Caravanbashi sat up straighter on his horse. Without turning, he told Qarasuvarli, "Turn the caravan towards Haji Gavar's caravansary in the lower quarter."

"Yes, Master."

Sarvan the camel driver rode up to Nazarali, who was leading Qotazli by a gaily decorated rope, a serious, determined expression on his face.

The Caravanbashi turned to look for Ibrahim and Sayyah. They should be somewhere in the middle of the caravan. Immediately sensing that the Caravanbashi was looking for him, Ibrahim galloped towards him.

His thoroughbred horse dancing beneath him, the Caravanbashi did not take his eyes off the caravan, and repeated to Ibrahim, "Do as I say. There's no need for you to go to the caravansary. Go straight home. After I've settled the caravan, I'll go to the palace into his presence. We have a lot to do before nightfall. Nazarali should take our things home. Keep an eye on everything. Have a rest yourself, and so should he," the Caravanbashi nodded towards Sayyah. Then, lowering his voice, he said, "You tell him what this is all about. I don't want to do it myself."

Without waiting for an answer, the Caravanbashi rode back to the head of the caravan. Ibrahim nodded to Sayyah and they rode their horses to the side of the road. Laden camel by laden camel, laden mule by laden mule, the caravan passed by. Joining the rear of the caravan, Sayyah saw that the head had already stepped through the city gates. The sound of the pipes and the hue and cry reverberated down the caravan.

Ibrahim and Sayyah turned together and set off down the Spring Road. This road would take them into the city by the small Spring Gate. When they entered through the gate, that part of the city was deserted (hadn't everyone poured down to the main gates to see the caravan arrive?) and they rode through the empty streets towards the Caravanbashi's house in the upper Qirxlar quarter. As they reached the house, the sun was just past its zenith.

Chapter 10

Dying Before Death

Tired to the bone as though they had lost their way and travelled far and wide, Sayyah lay still where he had collapsed onto the soft carpet in the large, warm guest room where the equally tired Ibrahim had taken him. It had been a long time since he was amongst such finery in such a well-appointed room. The Valley of the Sorcerers was comfortable, but the comfort here was of a different order. From every corner of this room wafted the warm, familiar scents of an intoxicating dream. Sleep easily got the better of him. At first he recoiled from the hustle and bustle, unaccustomed as he was to the usual noise of city life and the light shining through the thick glass of the windows. He half-closed his yes, his thoughts jumbled up. And in that intoxicatingly comfortable room, the familiar furious voices came to him again in his dreams.

"This isn't your place. Get out!"

"Go away. It's all your fault. Yours. This is your doing."

"Damn it. Damn it to the seventh level."[8]

His close friends of the day before now blocked the doorway to the tumbledown, snow-covered hut on top of the mountain and did not want to let him in. With curses and threats, they

---

8 In Sufi thought, there are seven levels of the self.

did not even give Sayyah the chance to speak. The snowflakes smothered last night's hope like pollen and punctured a hole in the darkness, showing the way in a flash of white. The hole of a thousand snowflakes, perhaps a hundred thousand, was the only way to the light.

Yesterday they executed the White Dervish. First they beat him unconscious, and then they crucified him. They looked with hatred at the remains of this near lifeless body. Summoning the last of his strength, the White Dervish tried to answer their questions. When he could get the words out, he answered with his voice. When he could not, he answered with his eyes. His eyes grew large and the onlookers were amazed that his eyes could be so downcast yet so attractive at such a difficult time. At the very end, his followers approached his crucified body one by one and whispered something to his half-alive, but still beautiful, eyes. After this, life at last left his body and his eyes were still.

What did his disciples say? They swore an oath to avenge him, but there was one of their number that they did not allow into their ceremony of vengeance. They slammed the door in his face. He went to a gloomy corner of the yard outside the hut. Tiny snowflakes caressed his face and clothes, turning him into a white statue. He stood stock still so he could hasten death out in the cold and had no intention of moving anywhere. He would stand until morning, until evening, until his last drop of strength was gone, until death. Sooner or later his comrades would have to listen to him. He had to learn the truth and he would learn it.

Rumours of revenge had already travelled down the mountain and reached the city. What revenge was there? For years he had slept in the same place in the hut. He had listened to them talking and teaching about the White Dervish's holes in the sky, about turning onto the path of the holes, about the possibility of travelling along that path, about the spirits making use of that opportunity. Together they had mourned and rejoiced. What vengeance were his disciple friends thinking about? What would they do and how would they do it? He remembered the Yellow Sayid's long, imposing face. The fear of vengeance filled even him and passed from his face to his small eyes. With spittle running down his chin, the Yellow Sayid said with his eyes, "Find out what's going on in their heads; come back safe and well. Safe and well, do you hear me? I need you safe and well."

The door to the hut was slowly pushed open, the sound muffled by the snow piled up outside. One by one, the White Dervish's disciples emerged. They were dressed in pure white garments down to their knees. There was a precipice behind the hut and they went and stood in a row along the top. They could not see the bottom of the valley below. They stood motionless, waiting. Only now did he understand their intentions and grasp the essence of their revenge. Standing soundless like statues, in their hearts they were summoning their spirits. Their aim was for their spirits to leave their bodies at the last moment. The White Dervish had invented this technique in his youth. Death came very slightly before death.

Sayyah was motionless, almost frozen solid in the near darkness, but continued to follow their every move. Unknown to himself, a half-smile settled on his lips, deepening the wrinkles on his face. So this is it. I'm the only one left. I was already alone. There will be no one but me.

These were the thoughts passing through his head as twenty-three bosom friends held hands and plunged down the precipice into the darkness of the void. Twenty-three sails opened inside the darkness. At first they fell like stones. No, at first they began to fly in circles like orderly cranes. After flying hand in hand like this for some time, like hawks that have seen their prey, they suddenly swooped down towards the bottom of the gorge. Not a word or sound came from any of the twenty-three as they hit the ground. They did not die when they hit, but as they flew in the air. This was how his twenty-three disciples avenged the White Dervish. There should really have been twenty-four of them.

He opened his eyes, startled by gentle knocking at the door. The person on the other side of the door cleared his throat. It was Khaja Ibrahim Agha.

"Come in," Sayyah said loudly, shaking the sleep from his eyes.

"Good evening," Ibrahim said as he came in, carefully protecting the flickering candle in his hand and placing it down. Light increased in the room. Shadows appeared on the long wall. Sayyah could not say what time the evening darkness had fallen. In the darkness, weariness had found a way to take him from his body.

"Greetings," Sayyah said, turning to face Ibrahim as he propped himself up on his side on a woollen bolster.

"Did you manage to get some rest?" Ibrahim asked kindly.

"What have I done that I should be tired? But I did rest. How are you?"

"I am fine. My master isn't back yet. He was to have gone to the palace into the presence of the Shah. He will come, God willing."

"The ruler of this land?"

"Of course. This caravan is his majesty's. He ordered the most expensive goods. Besides, there are a lot of gifts that should be presented personally to him. We have gifts received in his name."

"Very good, very good. May it go well. You know, Ibrahim

Agha, I think that our business will not work out tonight. I didn't at all like the colour of the sky just now. I can tell you that I need the sky to be the right colour. That is the main thing."

"What do you mean by the colour of the sky? When did you see the right colour?"

"I didn't. This is what my heart tells me. The sky since midday has not been what I want. Not what I want at all."

"What can I say?" Ibrahim was disappointed. "What can be done? Make yourself comfortable and do what you have to do to rest. I'll tell the master what you said. Is there anything you would like me to do for you?"

Sayyah thought, They might think that I'm spinning out the time on purpose in order to luxuriate in this splendour. Looking out of the window, he gazed attentively at the sky in an attempt to wipe the latest images from his mind. "No, it's not what I want at all. What can I do?" he said rather guiltily, looking out at the sky.

"What can I say? How will we know when the sky is the colour that you want?" Ibrahim asked hesitantly.

"I will know myself. You don't need to know. Be patient, Agha, patient. It's not up to me, you know," Sayyah replied, turning to face Ibrahim.

CHAPTER 11

Colour of the Sky

I t was already late by the time Ibrahim heard the Caravan-bashi outside. He quickly rose and went out to meet him. Servants were leading his horse away. The Caravanbashi's first question was, "Did you talk to him? What happened? What did he say?"

"We talked, Master, we talked. Let's go inside first. You'll get cold out here," Ibrahim replied.

The frost had begun to set in at night. They went from the cold yard into the warm family quarters where a young woman with a child of five or six in her lap was waiting impatiently for the Caravanbashi's return. When they saw him, they jumped up. The child wriggled out of his mother's arms and threw himself into his father's fond embrace.

"Come here, come here. Let's have a look at you! See how you've grown, thank God!"

"Thank God, thank God," Ibrahim repeated gladly.

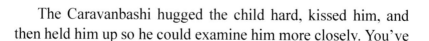

The Caravanbashi hugged the child hard, kissed him, and then held him up so he could examine him more closely. You've grown, your look is sharper, he thought to himself, and then put the lad down. The child, who had grown a lot heavier, clung to his father's leg.

The Caravanbashi walked slowly and carefully across the room so as not to dislodge the child, and sat down on the carpet next to the woman. Taking the woman's hand, he pulled her down next to him. He studied her carefully and then said gently, stroking her hand, "You haven't changed at all. How are you? There's something not right. It's been a long time, is that it?"

The woman hung her head in embarrassment or for another reason. Muttering something under her breath, she withdrew her hand from the Caravanbashi's and flushed bright red. "What did you say?" he asked, not wondering what it was all about.

In reply, the woman straightened the scarf over her long hair and again whispered something incomprehensible.

"She's asking if you want something to eat," Ibrahim translated, annoyed with the wife's mumbling.

"No, I don't. Vizier Mashdali fed me well at the palace." The Caravanbashi turned back to the woman. "No. I see you look well, but maybe a bit tired. Have you got your presents?"

Finding her tongue at last, the woman said, "Thank you, yes we have. I am a little tired. Last night I didn't sleep, as I thought you might come. I was waiting. I put him to bed," she said, nodding towards the child, "but whatever I did, I couldn't get to sleep myself."

As soon as the woman found her voice, what did the Caravanbashi remember? On a hot summer's day, quite unexpectedly, a messenger came from the Shah to say, "The Pivot of the Universe wants to see you." He had staggered to his feet, dressed, and forced himself in the direction of the palace. The Shah gave him a slave girl as a gift. His brother, the Emir of Kheyirabad, had sent him seven specially chosen beauties. The first time he laid his eyes on her, he saw a thin, sullen, taciturn girl on the short side. She suddenly raised her head, showing her large green eyes, and stared at him. She tried to conceal her waterfall of hair beneath a silk scarf, but did not always manage it.

Why on earth do I need this? God, what kind of a girl is she? he thought to himself, but lavished thanks on the Shah and left the palace, muttering under his breath, the girl behind him, as they slowly made their way home through the stifling streets. A year later their baby boy was born, and in keeping with the demands of his religion and his heart he made the girl his legal wife.

Pushing aside those recollections, the Caravanbashi said, "Go on and get some rest. I'll come soon." A gentle smile played on his lips, but he didn't look at the woman, rather at the carpet where she had been sitting. "Come over here and sit down where I can see you, Ibrahim Agha."

The woman took the child by the hand and was about to leave but the Caravanbashi hugged the boy once more and smoothed his hair. 'When you wake up tomorrow morning, old man, come and give me this year's report. Will you give it to me?"

The child's eyes shone with pride. He raised his head importantly, cast his father a look of love, and nodded. He ran after his mother, took her hand and, both pleased, they left the room together.

"What's up? Have the goods come?" the Caravanbashi asked Ibrahim as he warmly watched them go and made himself comfortable.

"They've come. Everything is where it should be. How are you? Did you see the Pivot of the Universe?"

"I did. I received his 'blessing.'"

"God be thanked a thousand times."

"That's enough about that. What about our business? What news?"

Ibrahim's voice changed and he said dully, "What news can there be? Our business is fine, but there is a but."

"What is it, this but?"

"He says the colour of the sky isn't right."

"The colour of the sky isn't right?" the Caravanbashi frowned in amazement.

"Yes, my lord. I don't think he's playing any tricks."

"Hmm, so what does the colour of the sky have to do with this, Ibrahim Agha?"

"It has something to do with it, sir. It seems that it does."

The Caravanbashi thought for a while. Ibrahim was sharp, and if he said that the sorcerer was not playing tricks then there was nothing untoward going on. But what did this colour business mean? What would they do?

"What should we do now?" the Caravanbashi asked.

"Wait, sir. What else can we do but wait?"

The Caravanbashi and Ibrahim talked some more about it. After their discussions, they decided to be patient a while longer and not bother Sayyah with questions until he spoke himself. Ibrahim looked with concern at the Caravanbashi. He looks tired, it would be good if he got some rest, he thought to himself, getting up. But as he was leaving he asked, "Did Vizier Mashdali ask you anything about me, sir?"

"Why should Vizier Mashdali ask about you, Ibrahim?" the Caravanbashi asked in reply.

"No reason, I just wondered if he remembered me. I'm talking about that journey."

"No, don't worry, he didn't ask."

"Thank you, sir. Sleep well. Get a good rest. You're worn out."

Vizier Mashdali is Vizier Mashdali; he's old and frail. Why would he remember you? You're a funny one, the Caravanbashi thought as Ibrahim left the room. Then the thin, wrinkled face of Vizier Mashdali with its wispy white beard appeared before his eyes.

Chapter 12
Young Mammadqulu Wants to be a Headsman

In that city close to God he would have to take his leave of his comrades-in-arms, of his beloved Shah with whom he had grown up, and of the white-bearded Vizier Mashdali who he could never repay. He would go to see Vizier Mashdali. He would sob and plead if necessary. He would apologise with great regret. "I am your eternal slave; you have been a father to me," he would say. He loved him more than the apple of his eye, his son, and would entrust his son to him. He would beg him to convey his request to the Shah, as his heart would not allow him to do it himself. He would try to capture the confused gaze of Vizier Mashdali, to get inside that gaze and find out what lay behind it.

Then he would go back home to the quiet, narrow, cobbled street, slim as a bird's neck, that wound upwards higher even than his house and ended he knew not where. First he would infuriate the beautiful Parnisa who would fling herself at his chest, desperate for good news. "It's not possible. They won't allow it. Just as I came together with the troops, I must leave with them too. There are other campaigns to come."

How the lovely Parnisa would take this, God alone knew. He

would drive her wild. After savouring her fury, he would reveal the truth—the truth! But where the truth lay, he couldn't say. The truth lay in the depths of Vizier Mashdali's surprised eyes or in his words, "I'll see what I can do. I don't know how I'm going to give the Pivot of the Universe this news," or in the decision that the Shah had not yet taken. Where did the truth lie? The only truth he knew was that he had already decided that he would not be going back with the troops. He could not be parted from Parnisa. Wasn't this really the truth? Of course, if this wasn't really the truth, then what was?

Agitated, Mammadqulu now began to think everything through. What stance would the Pivot of the Universe take towards him? Dark thoughts crept into his mind. He remembered what the Shah said when he was out for a stroll.

"Write this down, Scholar Sadraddin, write this down," he said to his scribe. "It took us just two hours to bring a city of this size to its knees. But the troops should be aware that these are our brothers and sisters in the faith. They went astray, so we gave them a slap in the face to bring them to their senses. This is our own country, our own people; there can be no question of plunder or the like. If anyone gets carried away with pillaging, or any complaint is made about a soldier, without me having even to open my mouth, Mammadqulu the Headsman will inflict punishment. This is his profession."

Sadraddin did not take his eyes off the quill. "Write this, too! If anyone is thinking of staying in this defeated city, a blemish will be upon all their descendants, because even the air we breathe here is bent double. The air, the stones, the water, the bread, everything that has seen defeat here has been emasculated. Only someone who does not love me could entertain such a thought."

Mammadqulu's request to the Shah spread through the air, from ear to ear, from house to house, corporal told corporal, centurion told centurion. Aristocrats, nobles, and heads of detachments froze in expectation. What punishment would the Shah mete out to his favourite headsman, if there would be a punishment at all? Maybe Mammadqulu would be granted his pig-headed wish to remain in this city and not leave with the troops? Maybe the Shah would turn a blind eye towards this unexpected request, maybe . . . Everyone understood this in their own way.

No one told Mammadqulu what the Shah had decided for several days. The poor man was wretched with anxiety. Of course, he had made a great mistake, but the die was already cast. He thought, There is Shahveran in the Shah's army who can replace me, so God willing there is nothing to stop him from letting me go. May God do as he will.

Mammadqulu had an assistant, an old slave, with whom he would share his concerns and anxiety, to whom he would open his heart, and whose advice he would seek. Nodding his dark head at the end of every conversation with Mammadqulu, this old slave always repeated his last words, "May God do as he will," and fell silent. But while fear was hidden in his watery eyes, he felt sorry for Mammadqulu, as he was the only person in the world to whom he felt bound from the heart. For many long years he had had no one else.

When he heard about the affair, the old slave was silent for some time. Looking askance, he said, "May God turn everything to the good." But he sounded so hopeless that Mammadqulu made a black mark in his heart and forbade himself to say a word about it to anyone else. He had no choice but to sit and wait for the Shah's decision.

At last, Vizier Mashdali found the moment to convey Mammadqulu the Headsman's request to the Shah, though he had never regretted anything so much in his life. For a long time he castigated himself. The Pivot of the Universe's eyes seemed to fly from their sockets and sting the vizier's eyes like a bee. How he scowled. The blow was completely unexpected. The fact that it came from his familiar servant, Mammadqulu the Headsman, only made him ten times more furious.

He said hoarsely, "Well, this headsman eventually had to show his base nature. What a shame, a great shame. So it no longer suits him to be in my service. Upon what or whom does he now rely? Do you know, Vizier? You must know; isn't he your man, this ignoble creature? You haven't forgotten how it was you who saddled us with him? He should have swung from the gibbet then. We did a bad deed when we took him into our service, tried to make a man of him. Now look at him!

"So what happened? If the headsman deserts the army during a campaign everyone will think they can go wherever they like. What else do you expect? Then what do you need me for? Why are you looking away? That's it, keep quiet. What can you say? Am I right or not? Maybe, Vizier, you have forgotten this one's life story? Wasn't it you who sadly told me of his valour in infancy as he wandered the mountains? Did he not send his mother to the next world? And this is how he repays my charity? You know who is to blame? Me. Of course, you keep quiet. What can you say after all? It's my fault, mine."

"Don't talk like that, light of my life. You are striking bitter blows to my heart. What can I say to you, who to me is God's equal? How could I, wretch that I am, know what an ingrate he is? How could I have known that he drank the milk of a dog? But I should have known! Of course, the fault is mine. I am ready for any punishment you deem necessary. He turned out to be a base wretch. You spoke true—he has gotten above himself and has gone bad. How could I have spoken up for him to you?" Vizier Mashdali could feel a cold sweat trickling down to his drawers.

The Shah glanced at Vizier Mashdali, and then continued in his fury, going straight for the kill. "That scoundrel, that traitor, even talks about Shahverdi's son? He advises me whom to appoint in his place! Vizier! I've no time to waste. He must be taught a lesson and everyone must see it. Come here and listen. Listen carefully to what I have to say."

As he said this, a winter blizzard flashed in the depths of the Shah's eyes. They shivered from the cold and froze over. The Shah's words to Vizier Mashdali came not from his mouth, but his eyes.

That evening, Vizier Mashdali carried a burden of both joy and fear in his heart as he entered the building where he lived. He had escaped the Shah's wrath without major injury—of course he gave thanks for that. But Vizier Mashdali knew that Mammadqulu would soon be coming to his house, as usual, to find out if the Shah had answered his request. He came quietly every day and left quietly. Today would certainly be no different.

To be on the safe side, as soon as he got home the Vizier called his chamberlain and gave him orders that no one was to be admitted to the courtyard that evening, and especially not to see him, since he had a bad headache. He said he must have caught a summer cold and would go to bed. Then thinking about something else, he gave another order, "Yesterday's servants are resting now, but get them up. Let there be a lot of servants on duty tonight, many of them in the courtyard. Close the doors and windows now."

With that, Vizier Mashdali went into the depths of the house. As he drew a strange breath, his chest wheezing, a long memory like an old carpet unrolled before his eyes. Like a blind man wafting away smoke, he drove away the sudden memory. Unfastening his clothes, he slipped under the wool blanket, pulling it over his head. Only then did he feel that he had told the chamberlain the truth, as he really did have a fever and had begun slowly to shiver. But the shivering was partly the result of nerves at the Shah's decision. This fever had washed him to his memory of a few moments ago and then brought him back beneath the woollen blanket.

This was what he remembered. One day, a servant came to Vizier Mashdali, who had been about to take to his bed, and brought him news that someone was at the door and wanted to speak to him on a very important matter.

"It's a young man, Master. His beard and moustache nearly cover his eyes. He looks like a bandit, but he won't give up and says you know him."

"Who is he? What's his name?" the vizier asked, bemused.

"I don't know, Master. He didn't say. Shall I ask him?"

"No, bring him here and let me see who it is. Whoever he is, whatever protection he is seeking, he must have a reason. Bring him here."

An imposing young man with a beard like a dervish followed the servant into Vizier Mashdali's room. Hard though the Vizier looked, he did not recognize the man. "Who are you? What do

you do? What is your lineage?" the Vizier asked, studying the
visitor with interest.

"Master, you knew my late father. He was a camel driver in
the Shah's caravan."

Just as Vizier Mashdali opened his mouth to ask "Who was
your father?" he was suddenly shaken by a vision. This gloomy,
hirsute young man seemed to split in two, and from inside
emerged the friend of his childhood, Qadirqulu the camel driver.
His stocky stature and gentle face were just as he remembered
from his long-gone youth. He stood to one side, leaning back
proudly with his hands interlinked behind his head, looking a
touch resentfully and sorrowfully at Vizier Mashdali. The vizier
looked longingly at his childhood friend. When he had had his
fill, he at last took his leave and Qadirqulu the camel driver left,
stepping back into the body of his son. This time Vizier Mashdali
did not ask a question, just sought confirmation, "Mammadqulu,
is it you?"

"Yes, it's me."

"It's you. Now I recognize you. What brings you here at this
late hour?"

"I have come to cast myself at your feet.. I am surrendering
myself to you, but my story is something else."

"What is your story, Mammadqulu? Come and sit down.
Would you like anything to eat or drink?"

"No, thank you. I don't want anything. If you hear me
out, that is enough for me. Listen to me and then make your
decision—am I guilty or not—and tell me."

Vizier Mashdali had, of course, heard that Mammadqulu had
become an outlaw, but he did not really know how or why. The
strangest fabrications had been woven so densely around this
incident that it was impossible to find the thread of truth. When
Mammadqulu went on the run, he gave no word, so people said

about him the first thing that came into their heads. What other people said was one thing, but what he said himself would be quite another. As Mammadqulu began to tell his story, the Vizier could not take his eyes off the young man, now a little older, whom he had known since he was a child. What the luckless Mammadqulu told him made the hairs on the back of his neck stand on end.

Mammadqulu really did narrate all that had happened to him, slowly, without emotion, looking at the ground, while Vizier Mashdali listened to him with the same forbearance. Late in the day when Mammadqulu's father, Qadirqulu, returned with the caravan from a long journey, bandits came to his home and killed him. He was a good man, a quiet man. He spent his life travelling from one land to another. It was a very murky murder and all the blame was pinned on the robbers.

According to another rumour, guides from Arabia, who had accompanied the caravan for part of the journey, had coveted his goods and money, and in the middle of the night entered his house in search of plunder and killed him. Sensing something was wrong, his father managed to send Mammadqulu, who was a young boy at that time, out of the house through the narrow backdoor to the yard just before the killers came. When the killers had completed their business with Qadirqulu, they supposedly subjected his wife to unbearable torture, demanding that she tell them where the gold was hidden. They did not get what they wanted, as the wife was too clever for them. She managed to trick them and ran to a neighbour, her husband's cousin, Zabulla, and the merchant saved her life.

But the years passed and the rumours spread until, like a bee making a beeline for a flower, they reached the ears of Mammadqulu, whose upper lip had yet to show signs of a moustache. At last, he heard all about it. The talk of plunder, of the caravan guides coming and robbing the house and killing the master were all lies. The truth was that Qadirqulu's wife plotted with Zabulla to kill him. The trap had been set a long time ago. They had fallen in love a many years prior and were awaiting this return with fear and trepidation, lest tales of their love, which would seem a bitter intrigue during his absence, should reach Qadirqulu's ears. This fear was not without foundation. Of course, the neighbours put two and two together, when night after night one neighbour hurried to the house of another.

Mammadqulu, who now had a shadow on his upper lip, heard all the rumours, whispers, and tittle-tattle. He was bound to be affected by the love affair between his mother and his father's cousin. He really suffered. He turned it over and over in his mind, until at last one night he called out hoarsely to his mother who was getting ready for bed in another room, "I want some water; bring me some water."

Mammadqulu crept after the woman as she took the water jug, and was right behind her as she reached the well in the yard. Sensing something, his mother turned her head. When she suddenly saw Mammadqulu, she was startled and asked pointlessly, "Mammadqulu, is that you?"

She looked hard into his stony face. Whatever was in her heart, she did not speak again, only murmured sorrowfully, "La ilaha illallah." (There is no god but God.)

At that moment, Mammadqulu struck her a powerful blow, sending her plummeting to the bottom of the well. Neither shouts nor groans came from the well. Without thinking about what he had done, Mammadqulu rushed to the neighbouring yard. He found the small gate hidden by briars and weeds in the wall between their yard and Zabulla's and pushed it hard. The gate opened without a creak or squeak.

During the hot summer nights Zabulla would stretch out on his mattress beside the pool in the courtyard. That night his snores were reverberating around the yard to the disgust of the roses timidly growing along the wall. Mammadqulu clutched the dagger in his hand and plunged it right into Zabulla's heart. Summoning his entire being, Zabulla's soul came out through his eyes. He opened them for one last time, wide and with a hint of surprise, before he closed them forever. When he saw Mammadqulu looming over him, he let out an ah of surprise as blood trickled from his mouth. He wanted to summon his last strength, but whatever he tried he could not raise his head. What strength he had ebbed away, but a cheerful smile settled on his lips. After all life had gone from his body, that smile still remained.

After this bloody event, no tidings came of Mammadqulu for a long time. He became an outlaw, roaming the mountains. No more was seen of him. He shunned everyone. Some years flew by, while others dragged. This life changed his appearance, and now here he was sitting opposite Vizier Mashdali. What did he want, this poor wretch?

"I want to return to the world, Master. I want to enter the Shah's service. For the sake of my father, petition on my behalf to the Pivot of the Universe; he will listen to you." Mammadqulu finished his long, painful discourse with this entreaty, raised his head for a moment to look into the Vizier's surprised face, then bowed his head and was quiet.

A deep silence fell. Vizier Mashdali was plunged in thought. Then he asked Mammadqulu, "A servant of the Shah, you say? What sort of servant?"

The answer made his hair stand on end. "I would be his headsman, Master."

Mammadqulu spoke those words in a single breath and then relaxed. He went on as though to himself, "I'm tired of roaming the mountains. I'm oppressed by this life of wandering. Shadows follow a man morning and night. These cruel shades show no mercy and pierce my eyes in the darkness of the night. I have no peace at their hands. I sought refuge with you, Master, my father's friend. You wished each other well and broke bread together. God, and now you, alone know that I bear no guilt for what happened. My hands are clean before God and the Shah.

"My father, my breadwinner, came to me every night in my dreams. 'You are not my son if you can sleep at night when your father's murderers enter his bed chamber every evening, trample on his honour, and abuse his name. How can you bear this, my son Mammadqulu?' my father's spirit would ask me. But since that night, he no longer comes to me in my sleep, no longer asks anything of me. He must be at peace."

Vizier Mashdali's heart was touched. As he saw Mammadqulu out, he gave him his word that he would find the right moment to convey his request to the Shah. "Maybe something will work out," he said in his heart and out loud.

Mammadqulu's eyes shone. "Shall I come for an answer the day after tomorrow?" he asked. When the vizier said yes he felt calm at last, and left the Vizier's house saying prayers for him in his heart.

Much later, when he watched Mammadqulu at work, Vizier Mashdali was amazed by his zeal. But Mammadqulu had an old slave as his assistant, and when Vizier Mashdali heard his words, his amazement evaporated. The old slave said, "When this man tortures the guilty and the innocent, cuts off their heads and suffocates children with such zeal and enjoyment, it makes him forget his own sorrow. His sorrow is great; it is not easy to bear. In playing like this with death, in hanging people and chopping off their heads, he manages to wipe away the gloom of that great sorrow and loneliness. He drives away his sorrow, if indeed that can be done."

The old slave was worldly wise. When he heard those words, Vizier Mashdali bit his lip and thought, Hmm, there is some truth in that.

Chapter 13
On the Trail
of the White Dervish

"**O**h God! Beloved God, help us. Help your world that all things continue to flow as they always have, that the rivers of this world flow as they always have down to the sea, that the trees, plants, and flowers strive towards the sun, that the rains fall from the sky to the earth and not the other way around, that the shadows protect people from the sun, that love should have a thousand and one names, that life should come before death, and that the living should not leave the right path leading to their end.

"Oh, God, help us lest the minutes, hours, and days retreat within themselves, lest they fight one another and are lost. May they follow each other steadily and patiently."

Sayyah was staring out through the window of the Caravanbashi's first-floor guest room, chanting under his breath to make sure that no changes, earthquakes, or the like had yet occurred to disrupt the course of time. The minutes and hours went by steadily and calmly like the guardsmen, their swords unsheathed, who marched back and forth outside the Shah's palace. Nothing changed anywhere. The sky still did not turn the colour that was so important to him. Had he been asked what the colour was that would allow him to get down to work, he could not have answered. He would feel it in his soul. It would tell him that the long-awaited time had come at last, the hours and minutes had merged, a storm had broken within time, and the colour of that storm had risen to cover the skies. But he did not know what the colour was, its name, or how it could dare to cover the skies.

A time of waiting can be finer than the end awaited. Long nights, sweet nights, and on one such night Ibrahim and Sayyah were sitting facing one another on the guest room's flowered carpet, propped up on bolsters, their knees just touching. Ibrahim hardly dared to breathe for fear of breaking Sayyah's train of thought and stopping the conversation. What he was hearing interested him greatly.

"You heard right. After the White Dervish's execution, his disciples committed suicide. Yes, this suicide was linked with the execution of the master who had set our souls on fire. But after the suicides, the province's Great Clerical Council was terrified. They wanted to investigate the reason for the suicides.

"The Yellow Sayid wanted to see me. They took me to him. This was no longer the formidable, authoritative Yellow Sayid that I knew who boldly opposed the White Dervish while beating his chest and breathing fire. This was an old man with sweat dripping down his wrinkled face, his eyes unable to settle, a desperate servant of God. He asked me a couple of things about my fellow disciples. I shed some light on some of the darker moments. The Yellow Sayid asked me again, 'Why did you not end your life with them?'"

"It is not my life. The Almighty giveth and the Almighty taketh away."

"You have answered well. My hope is in you. You must reject the teachings of the White Dervish before the Great Council.

Shall you do it?"

"I will reject his teachings. What more should I do?"

"You must deny that you were his disciple."

At this, I was silent.

"Why are you silent?" The Yellow Sayid's eyes could not concentrate on my face and failed to read my decision.

"That night, for the first time since I left the Wheel of Fate, I had a dream. I saw twenty-three people throw themselves from the top of a mountain into an abyss to end their lives, but before they hit the ground one of them, whose white clothes became wings, flew up like a white bird and settled right in front of me in my hiding place. This was one of my favourite disciples, my friend. The White Dervish was always especially affectionate towards us. This person said to me in my sleep, 'Of course, you did not fly with us for a reason. You know too that the White Dervish died in body but not in soul. At this hour his soul is being reborn somewhere else. His heart is already beating. Listen, can you hear the beat?'

"I suddenly realised that as soon as I fell asleep, a thundering had continued unabated in the skies above me. He continued, 'You have been charged with finding him.'

"'But how shall I do that?' I asked.

"'I swear to you by the soul of the holy teacher. Wherever you place your foot every day, you will be moving towards him. Every night you will have strange, wondrous dreams. Your dreams will take you from village to village, from camp to camp, from land to land. The night when you do not dream you will know that you have reached the place you seek. When you wake up the next morning, you will see him at your side.'

"'The White Dervish?'

"'Yes, the White Dervish.'

"'How will I know him? What will our meeting be like?'

"'You'll wake up and see him. He will say, 'Welcome.' Then you must reply, 'I bring joy.'

"'Welcome, I bring joy?'

"'It's time for me to go. They will soon reach the bottom of the valley. Of course, you will do as I say. But you should be aware of this; it's important that you know. This is how he wanted things to be.'

"When he had finished, my dear friend looked at me for the last time, before the wind filled his white clothes. Like a bird he soared into the sky, then plummeted into the abyss and was no more. At sunrise, in just my woollen tunic with a staff in my hand, I left that accursed city. I went wherever my feet took me. That journey was truly long."

Sayyah the Sorcerer broke off, lost in gloomy thought. Ibrahim was still afraid to utter a word, so he kept silent. After a good while passed in this way, Ibrahim plucked up courage to whisper, "And did you find him?"

Sayyah answered flatly, "I found him. Of course, I did."

"That road must have been very difficult."

"I had to pass many trials in order to come out alive. But, come what may, I was determined that I would find him. I would ask for my sins to be forgiven. Although during our conversation the Yellow Sayid said to me, 'You know you have not a grain of guilt in this matter. Our religion had so entered your soul, so no matter how much you wanted to, you could not continue. If anyone bears any guilt in this it is that wanderer who calls himself the White Dervish and bewitched his disciples into loving him. He is not even from these parts. He is said to be from a place by the name of the Invisible Mountain.'

"'Why the Invisible Mountain?' I couldn't help asking.

"The Yellow Sayid was silent for a moment and didn't hear. Something passed through his mind and he couldn't make up his mind whether or not to tell me. His eyes darted hither and thither. Finally, he found strength from somewhere and began to speak.

"'Far, far away lies a strange land. For a while it is visible to the eye, but then it becomes invisible. No one knows where so great a land, so many villages, towns, roads, and pathways disappear to. Then five years later, or perhaps ten or fifty, they appear once more, as though they had never disappeared, and the people are carrying on with their lives. The people of this land do not know when they will disappear, whether they hide in the skies or on earth, or when they will re-emerge from their hiding place.

"'There is a valley near their capital. The mountain road runs past it. There is a mountain near one section of that road. No one knows if that mountain really exists or not, because it cannot be seen. Those who have reached the summit say it is as though they were climbing emptiness up to the sky. Below the mountain, a valley opens up that is called the Valley of the Sorcerers. All the sorcerers of the world have gathered there. They have formed a circle. Amongst themselves they call it the Circle of Darkness, and they try with all their might to bring darkness into our world. If the circle closes, then they might accomplish their aim. At present, one link is missing from this circle. All the might of magic in the world is gathered in that valley. Now listen carefully to what I am about to say.'

"'Yes, please continue. I am all ears,' I said.

"The Yellow Sayid continued sadly, 'The White Dervish has returned to his roots, to his source. He has found a new body and has returned to our world. He is a baby at the breast. Would I not know the beating of his heart?'

"The Yellow Sayid paused and really did prick up his ears to listen to a sound that only he could hear. I heard no sound, no voice. 'Of course, he has been reborn. He is the missing link in the valley's Circle of Darkness. If that link is in place, we are lost. The world will fall into the hands of the sorcerers. Darkness will rule and there will be hell on earth.'

"'How will this happen, Master?' I asked.

"'Very easily. In his Detailed History of Miracles Sheikh Asrari Imangetirmish writes that the last miracle in our world was the Holy Koran, which our beloved Prophet received from God and gave to all mankind. There is no place in our world for any more miracles. If the forces of evil in our world unite, they can wipe the Holy Koran from the memory of mankind. This will be both the last miracle and the end of the world. A black curtain will fall over the entire earth. The White Dervish said that because the Word was in the beginning before everything was made, the Word is at the end too. The circle has been closed. No one knew of this beforehand.'

"I dared to interrupt him, 'Master, how can it be that the Word is at the end? I did not hear the White Dervish say this, and we have not yet reached the end.' The Yellow Sayid again looked at me sadly. This time his face looked like a child's, his eyes stopped darting hither and thither and fixed on a single point—my face—and at last he gave me this reply, 'We did not know about this, no one knew. The White Dervish could not bear it and spoke out. You know he could never keep a secret in his heart. Maybe he was waiting for the right time to tell you, but he told us that the end has already come, the final Word has already been spoken. We are living after the end, you see.'

"When the Yellow Sayid saw that I was thinking hard, he changed the subject and gave me my last task. 'The White Dervish will appear in his homeland, the Valley of the Sorcerers. You must find him. It is you that knows his heart and can stand in the way of the last link being fitted into the Circle. You know what to do. Kill him! We must kill him anew every time. He will be reborn and we must kill him. Now go. Go! My secretaries will give you whatever you need. You will always be under the watchful eye of the Great Council. May you be in God's care, too.'"

Ibrahim was flabbergasted. His mouth fell open in amazement as he listened. When Sayyah paused for breath, Ibrahim leapt in with a question, which immediately turned into several questions at once.

"Forgive me, but you said, or rather the Yellow Sayid said, that our land and the people who live here can sometimes be seen and sometimes disappear. How can that be? I have lived in this land all my life and never felt anything. No one has felt anything. Can there be a time when the world around us cannot see us? Where do we disappear to then? Why do we not know this?"

At first, Sayyah did not know how to answer, but Ibrahim was not set on getting a reply. As Sayyah shrugged his shoulders, Ibrahim thought to himself, What does he know? These are the words of the Yellow Sayid.

But Sayyah did not leave his questions unanswered. He thought carefully before saying, "First, neither you nor I know whether the Yellow Sayid was talking about your country or another one. Second, even now, no one can see the people of this land or us ourselves! Third, maybe that invisible land lies near the Invisible Mountain and that now is the time for it to be invisible!"

While Ibrahim reported to the Caravanbashi every evening about Sayyah, he did not go into detail of what or whom they talked about. Ibrahim had always been interested in intelligent conversation and now thought in his heart of hearts that it would be good if Sayyah stayed a little longer in this house. Who did he find in his teacher's place in the Valley of the Sorcerers? He had to know. Had Ibrahim seen this person when he went down into the valley? It would be really interesting to know what happened to the soul of the body that had received the White Dervish's soul. Where had it gone? Did the White Dervish recognise his old pupil Sayyah? Now the meaning of his name was clear. He had become a wanderer in order to find the White Dervish. So if that was the case, then . . .

Several days passed in this way. But one morning when Ibrahim came to Sayyah's room carrying his breakfast on a copper tray, the sorcerer had already gotten up, dressed, and was leaning out of the window, staring up at the sky. His heart jumped. Putting the tray down, he went up to Sayyah and, following his line of vision, began to look too. Ibrahim could not make out anything special in the sky, just greyish-black clouds, but Sayyah was really tense. He gave no acknowledgement of the khaja's presence.

"Good morning. What's going on? Is it good?" Ibrahim asked.

"It's good of course; good morning to you. This evening, if God wills, we should reach our goal. The colour has been seen in the sky. Tell your master that he has to return home just as it begins to fall dark."

Ibrahim felt both happy and sad as he went down to the inner chambers and found the Caravanbashi just sitting down to breakfast. When he gave him the news, the Caravanbashi did not react, but Ibrahim saw a sudden flash of light in the depths of his eyes that just as suddenly disappeared.

"I will come home at the appointed hour. Tell him—no, don't tell him anything. I'll tell him myself this evening. Be careful. Make sure that none of the servants remain in the house. There will be the three of us—him, you, and me, no one else. And tell her," the Caravanbashi nodded towards the women's quarters, "that she and the child should go to bed as soon as I come home. They must not go upstairs. I must now go into the Shah's presence. I'm late; I'll see how I can excuse my tardiness."

Without eating any of his breakfast, the Caravanbashi rose, straightened his clothes, and put on his cloak. Without saying another word or even glancing in Ibrahim's direction, he left the house. The groom had already led his thoroughbred horse out, and he leapt into the saddle. Instead of cantering out at his usual steady pace, the Caravanbashi cracked his whip so hard that the startled horse bolted for the gate, galloped out of the yard, and flew down the road. Ibrahim could hear the horse snorting a long way away beyond the Water Garden.

CHAPTER 14
The White Dervish in the Valley of the Sorcerers

Ibrahim did not take his eyes off the gate until the Caravanbashi had galloped through and disappeared from view. I've
got time before evening, he thought. Of course, he could
have learnt a lot from Sayyah, but the matter would be resolved
this evening, with God's mercy, and the Caravanbashi would
meet the soul of his father, Mammadqulu the Headsman.

Ibrahim believed that this was within Sayyah's powers.
His hour would come this evening. Of course, he would write
down his conversations with Sayyah later. It would not be a bad
thing to write down this conversation in nastaligh[9] and to add
the manuscript to his small home library of books that had been
carefully collected from towns, countries, corners, and quarters.
Sayyah would clearly leave tomorrow for his own land, back
to the Valley of the Sorcerers. When would Ibrahim ever meet
anyone of such knowledge and learning again?

As he did early every morning, Ibrahim gave the servants
their orders and arranged the work so that as darkness fell not
one of them would be in the house. Then he went into the inner
chambers, found the lady of the house, and had a quiet talk with
her. Then he went up to the first floor to Sayyah's room and

9 Nastaligh is a style of calligraphy of the Arabic script.

89

knocked softly at the door.

The sorcerer's voice came from inside, "Come in."

Ibrahim opened the door just wide enough to slip inside. From the empty dishes on the tray, he realised that Sayyah had already eaten his breakfast, drunk his tea, and was now sitting in the corner chanting to himself.

"I'm not disturbing you, am I?" Ibrahim asked gently.

"No, you're not." Sayyah saw that Ibrahim didn't know whether to sit or stand, so he gestured to the floor. "Sit down. If you have no other important work, sit down. The time will pass more quickly. There's still some time to go until evening."

Ibrahim took two bolsters from the bed, gave one to Sayyah, and put the other opposite him before sitting down cross-legged. There was just enough room for a salver between the two of them.

"Would you like anything?" Ibrahim asked, propping himself up on the soft bolster. "Sherbet? Maybe some fruit?"

"No, thank you. I have eaten my fill," Sayyah replied.

An awkward silence fell, which was finally broken by Ibrahim. "I told my master what you said. He said that as soon as darkness draws in he will be home."

"Good. Today we will complete this matter, come what may. I have already become a burden, staying here so long."

"Not at all, not at all. Don't say that. I've enjoyed the opportunity to talk to you."

The silence returned. It was as though Ibrahim had turned into a small, self-conscious child and didn't know how to begin the conversation. He resolved to come right out with a question that had troubled him for a long time. He had been given the tail of the mystery, and now he could see the whole body in the distance and was shaking like a leaf. "Tell me, who was the person who received the White Dervish's soul?"

Sayyah was expecting the question. He smiled, creasing all

the lines of his face. "You haven't guessed?"

He was about to say "No, I haven't guessed," but without knowing why, he clamped his lips shut before the words were out of his mouth. Ibrahim frowned like someone who had just remembered something, as he saw in Sayyah's eyes a young, familiar face looking back gently at him. He realised that, of course, he should have guessed. It was him, who else could it be? The young sorcerer who met him in the valley and took him to Sayyah, who spoke to Sayyah and welcomed him so warmly, of course, it was him. This certainty soothed his uneasy soul and mind. Ibrahim relaxed and even blushed as a warm smile spread over his face.

"You say you've guessed?" Sayyah was watching him with interest, but his voice seemed to come from a long way away, from the Valley of the Sorcerers.

"Yes, I've guessed," Ibrahim replied wearily.

"He told me the name of the meeting. It was still dark all around, but the darkness was slowly taking on light. For the first time that night I did not dream. This was the first time in all the long years that I had been on the road that I did not dream. It was the night that my beloved friend the martyr had told me of. I opened my eyes and saw him over me. He looked very gently at me.

"'Welcome,' he said softly. I was so amazed by the beauty of his voice that I forgot the name of our meeting. Though the voice has gone, I can still feel its mournful vibrations. 'Welcome,' he repeated. Then seeing that I could not utter a sound, he said softly, 'I bring joy.' Of course, I was then even more certain that the soul of the White Dervish was in the body before me."

CHAPTER 15
Light Is of Darkness, Darkness Is not of Light

Sitting in his usual spot, the White Dervish had changed his behaviour. How many times he turned his face up from the Valley of the Sorcerers towards the Invisible Mountain, gazing at it. Who he was looking for in that white storm he alone knew. He fixed his eyes to the road. Dark thoughts flooded his mind. He could not get rid of them no matter what he did.

Towards evening, the sorcerers took up their usual positions in the valley. The day had passed from life like all the other days. Once more there was the warmth of springtime, the singing of the birds, the embracing of the leaves of the apple, pear, and cherry trees, the twisting and turning of the crooked trunks of the grapevines, and the amazing sight of the flowers of the pomegranate tree on branches sagging with the weight of ripe fruit. Beyond the valley these gifts had their own seasons and you could not see blossoms and fruit together, but here everything was in one place in the same season to meet the sorcerers' needs.

Of course, there was no other place like it on Earth. The very existence of this place was without doubt a miracle. The inhabitants of this miracle lived deep within the miracle, waiting for the time when a voice deep within their souls spoke to them.

Every sorcerer was a prisoner of his inner voice. The voices had so far said only this, "Be patient, the time will come, don't hurry." The rhythm of these words beat in their souls.

The White Dervish felt the cool breeze on his face as darkness fell. The few stars in the sky twinkled at each other and hesitantly began to show their light to those watching. Were these stars not a sign that beyond the curtain of darkness was an abundance of bright light? Of course, they were a sign. Wherever they could, the stars broke through the curtain. They directed their melancholy gazes, full of questions, from one star to another.

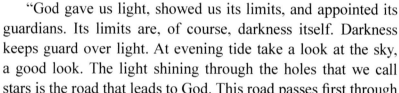

"God gave us light, showed us its limits, and appointed its guardians. Its limits are, of course, darkness itself. Darkness keeps guard over light. At evening tide take a look at the sky, a good look. The light shining through the holes that we call stars is the road that leads to God. This road passes first through darkness. So the road of darkness is the road to God. Mark my words."

"It's Satan's road!"

"It's God's road! Darkness is arrayed in rows along the road leading to light."

"They don't understand. They don't want to understand at all. They cannot understand the wisdom of darkness. They do not realise that only the darkness can bring you to the light. My beloved God, is it worth explaining to them this simple truth?" The White Dervish was starting to feel tired.

"Whatever will be will be. They need my head? Well, let them have it. Hasn't this been my cherished dream these long

years? They struggle for the body, the corporeal. So be it. I am
sick and tired of them. Dear God, I ask of you only this—that I
might join you, dissolve in you. I am in a bad way now. Send my
spirit to this earth again later."

"It's Satan's road and you are his messenger! You are the
messenger of darkness. You have no shame, calling yourself the
White Dervish. Have you ever stood on the road that leads to
God? Have you?"

"No, they cannot be allowed to absolve me, to have pity on
me. Then I would become one of them! No, never! Death, only
a fatwa for my death!"

The White Dervish made one last hopeless attempt to die.
"Our world is seen as one that lies within darkness, not light.
Light is of darkness, darkness is not of light. In the beginning
there was darkness. Light came from within it."

"Nonsense! Rubbish!"

"This person is casting doubt on light, on the truth. Your
words came out of your mouth, not your heart. Ask for God's
forgiveness!"

"What is this truth that you know?" the White Dervish's
voice roared amidst the hubbub of voices.

The Yellow Sayid came forward. He adjusted his robe over
his skinny shoulders. With a simplicity that delighted him,
bringing to life his shadow on the wall, he took a deep breath
and gave the following answer to the White Dervish's question,
"The truth is that you and I, now, at this hour and in this place,
are facing each other, listening to each other, and if we wanted
to we could even touch each other."

"Each other's bodies, yes, but each other, no. Not at all!
What you say is not the truth. Of course it's not. The truth is that
in their own worlds our souls hate each other."

"Our souls are in our bodies, nowhere else. When we die,

only our souls leave our bodies. If I am in good health, my soul cannot be anywhere other than within me."

"No, that is not true. Our souls are a long, long way away from us, and there they are but our shadows. I want to bring my shadow here to join my soul to my body." The White Dervish had a sudden thought. "I have strayed again from the path of my death. Let it be, but I will speak."

"The soul's place is here," the Yellow Sayid continued. "Do you know that it has become more difficult to breathe here without one's soul? If I could return our souls here our soil, mountains, rocks, and every living thing would be revived, new strength would come to our world. Our world is weak because our souls have disappeared. Worlds that have their souls within them are fighting with us. We simply are not aware of this yet. Only with the strength of our souls will we be able to fight this war."

"Be quiet! Not another word!"

"Be patient! Evil is speaking through this man's lips. Satan has entered his heart." The Yellow Sayid raised his hand in the air as he made his final accusation. Then, with the same hand he drove away a distant memory of the source of the discord between the two men that were trying to block his vision.

A noble friendship began in the distant years of their youth before their teacher, Sheikh Manuchohr ibn Sadiq, made his discovery of "the full moment." Did that full moment divide the two young men who so honestly loved each other? Sadly it did, as step by step, breath by breath, they became the enemies that they are today.

The White Dervish summoned the last scraps of strength from deep within his body. They came together in his weak, wracked frame, and he managed to say, "He who sees only the light cannot know its value. Your words are not sincere. I have nothing more to say."

For the first time, the White Dervish was lost in the stars. His self had disappeared, dissolved into one of the stars, a particle of light. His eyes searched for the path but could not find it. After he turned into light, his path was no more. Your path is the path of light that envelops everything, if it can be called a path. The bodies of the Yellow Sayid and the famous, glorious members of the Great Clerical Council who looked at him with such malice remained in the darkness that separated the stars. There was no path. Light was all around.

Chapter 16
Searching for the Spirit of Headsman Mammadqulu

Sayyah the Sorcerer concealed his unease with the long conversation. Khaja Ibrahim was struck by the thought that Sayyah might be so tired of his questions that he would not have the strength to summon the spirit of the Caravanbashi's awful father when evening came.

"What is it that we call a star?" Sayyah was just getting into his stride. "Is it a hole in the darkness that lets in light? It is the bright light, the endless light, behind the worn-out darkness. What is a star? A star is not really light; it is pieces of darkness amongst the display of light. A star is darkness itself. What is Satan? Is he not an angel who recognizes no one but his beloved God and nothing, even if it is against God's will? The holy teacher said that in his heart, apart from love for God, was even more love for God.

"The Yellow Sayid asked what a star was. The White Dervish replied, 'The stars are particles of the immense, infinite light that reach us. Today they have the strength to hold up the heavy cloak of darkness. The day will come when these particles can no longer hold up the weight of the magnificent darkness. This darkness will settle like a cry lightly, but inexorably, on the

earth, and we shall all be crushed beneath that cry.' This is what
the White Dervish said and he did not blaspheme."

Confounded, Ibrahim opened his mouth to ask something,
but Sayyah impatiently cut him off. "You want to ask why the
Yellow Sayid showed so much zeal? He and the White Dervish
were both disciples of Master Sheikh Manuchohr bin Sadiq at
one time. Their paths diverged later. The Yellow Sayid was a
keeper of secrets. He never revealed them, which is why he was
so merciless towards those who did. But the White Dervish . . .
whatever was in his heart he revealed on his tongue. He did not
keep the secrets of the time of solitude, and joyfully shared with
us his conversations with his beloved God. That's why he really
didn't like him. Do you know who the White Dervish was?"

"Who he was?" Ibrahim repeated Sayyah's question in a
whisper.

"Ibrahim Agha, the White Dervish is God's secret keeper.
He is God's only secret keeper. He knows his revelations. One
of his discoveries about ways of dying, made shortly before
his death, is priceless. The Yellow Sayid could be only God's
friend; he could not be his secret keeper. God's secret keeper
has taken his last breath before reaching God, before dissolving
within him. The last moment. Do you understand who the White
Dervish is?"

"I understand, I understand. Take a rest. You're tired and it
will soon be evening. Don't you want to rest or to have something
to eat?" Ibrahim was trying to change the subject because he was
so frightened by what he had heard.

"No, thank you," Sayyah said, sighing deeply and turning
to Ibrahim. "I'm not tired at all. It was you who wanted to hear
these things, wasn't it?"

"Yes, how did you know?" admitted Ibrahim, surprised.

"From your eyes. This is our last evening together. You

asked with your eyes and I answered with my tongue. Do you know anything about the love between the eyes and the tongue?" Sayyah narrowed his eyes so that they were almost invisible.

Evening drew in quickly, word by word and sentence by sentence. Whatever was outside the window passed from light to darkness. Although the Caravanbashi hadn't come home yet, he would be there any minute. Regardless of what they were talking about, these two men were each impatiently awaiting his arrival and gradually moving into an altered state.

When the Caravanbashi rode into the dark courtyard, only Ibrahim was there to meet him at the foot of the steps. Everything was as they had agreed that morning—the servants had already gone to their own quarters, and the watchmen quickly bolted the gate after the Caravanbashi and then melted away. All was quiet indoors. There was no sign of his wife or child. They had long since retired to the inner quarters and taken to their beds.

"Would you like something to eat, sir?" Ibrahim asked.

"No, I'm not hungry."

The Caravanbashi went into the large room on the right. He sat cross-legged in his usual corner, piling up the bolsters and cushions in case he wanted to lean back later. "What news, Ibrahim Agha?" he asked, turning to him. "Are you ready? If you only knew how I've been longing for evening. By God, it got dark so late you wouldn't think it was winter. What have you been doing?"

"Nothing, Master. We talked about this and that. Time passed very quickly. What do you think? Shall I go and get him? You have been waiting for a long time."

"Yes, go," the Caravanbashi said, hanging his troubled head, lost in thought.

May God hear my voice this time, may he grant my desire, whatever the cost. He had longed for this meeting with his father all his life, the man who stood watching him in all his dreams as though deaf and dumb. This meeting that would change the rest of his life. He had many things to ask him, many whys and wherefores to put to him, many secrets would be revealed. But the most important why was not why he had cast him into the care of his old grandmother and disappeared to God knows where. He would never allow himself to summon his father's spirit so impatiently just for that. His main aim was to calm his spirit, to give him peace. How many years had the spirits of his ill-fated brother and father not been at peace? Of course, after the meeting the spirits would find peace in that world. He prayed that they would.

Ibrahim, followed by Sayyah with a bundle in his hand, came quietly into the room. "Good evening. Are you ready, Master?" Sayyah asked in greeting.

"Good evening to you too. I'm ready." The Caravanbashi made to get to his feet. "Tell us where we should sit. Maybe—"

"Sit down, sit down. That's a good place for you, don't worry. Ibrahim Agha, you go and sit behind the Master. I will be over here. I demand only silence of you. You must not utter a word. When it is time, I will give you a sign. But until I give the sign, only silence. There's nobody about?"

Ibrahim reassured him that nobody indoors or out would interrupt them. Sayyah then gestured with his hand for the men to sit down. The Caravanbashi sat in his place and Ibrahim made himself comfortable a little behind him. Sayyah moved to the far side of the room and turned to face them. A candle in a holder stood on a small table in the middle of the room. Sayyah struck a flint, lit the candle, and returned to his place. The candle's light shone like a red line. The flame did not flicker but stood upright. Sayyah studied the vertical flame in silence for a long time. The two people in the opposite corner of the room disappeared in the gloom. They forgot themselves as they tensely followed every movement of Sayyah's, not only with their eyes, but with every muscle in their bodies, hardly daring to draw breath. Total silence swept the room.

Standing in one corner, Sayyah untied the bundle he had brought with him. He took out a prayer mat, unrolled it on the floor, and sat on it cross-legged, crossing his hands so that they rested on opposite knees.

What's he about to do? If he gets up and starts to spin like the others, nothing's going to happen. He won't come. I can feel it in my heart. He won't come. If he was going to come, he would have come that time when the sky was clear, full of stars above our heads, and that astrologer danced and spun and whirled. He would have brought out the tongue of a snake. It won't work this time either. Dancing and spinning won't make it work. If it doesn't work this time, then that means it is God's will. It's a sign. It's impossible to try anymore. This is the end of the affair. What's done is done. The arrow once shot does not return to the bow. Whatever will be will be. This is the counsel, but I will take my vengeance.

With these thoughts running through his head, the Caravanbashi watched as Sayyah put his head in his hands and rocked to and fro as he sat, chanting something under his breath. His voice was very low, barely audible. He had to concentrate very hard to make out even one word. Just as he thought he had a word, it slipped out of his hands and disappeared into the air.

Sayyah seemed to ask himself a question first and then to answer it.

"Which road shall we take? I don't know. There are many roads that we could take . . ."

He rocked to and fro again and fell silent. Then he asked himself another question. "What colour shall we cover ourselves in? 'I don't know. All the colours have merged. You can't distinguish them.'"

Again he fell silent. Again he rocked to and fro. Again he asked and answered his own question. "Whose tears have you wiped away in this world? No one's. So no tears have flowed into this world . . ."

This time he did not fall silent, but raised his voice so that not only he but the Caravanbashi and Ibrahim could hear. He sounded as though he had set out on a rocky road. The whisper became silence, the silence became a sob, and the sob suddenly became a decorous shout. "Stop, drop your hands! Come out of your shadow. If you are thinking of the moment to come and the one after that, then pin your hopes on the good of this evening, not the harm. But if you fly away, whirling over your tomorrow, with the bitter foretaste of the return of your yesterday, your head to one side and your body to the other, then remember this and don't forget. Don't come before my eyes!"

Sayyah said the last words in a different way, singing them in a rich voice, and then continued as before. "Come and free us of thoughts of this body trembling from excitement. You will not be able to keep the seaweed company at the bottom of the sea. What are you grieving for? Whatever will be will be. At last we must know. No, we must understand. No, we must perceive for ourselves that dry bodies do not hold the spirit."

Here Sayyah paused for breath again. Then, almost sobbing, but in a fine voice he said, "I have been weeping; don't be stubborn, come."

As he said these words, Sayyah really did shed some tears.

He wiped his eyes with the back of his hand, spreading the tears all over his face, and continued. "This winter night that does not warm you at all seems to come out from this confusion of voices, this riot of colour. If it can, it comes out, if it cannot, it looks at you from afar, unable to caress your beautiful face with its plaintive breath. Your shadow throbs and whispers, only your heart is aware of that whisper. Your shadow is whispering its love to your body . . ."

Sayyah again paused for breath. This time a deep entreaty could be heard in his voice. "For your own death's sake, don't be lazy, come."

Sayyah's body, which had been rocking back and forth all the time he had been speaking, suddenly shot bolt upright and he drew breath. He did not know where the enchanting voice came from, from his heart or whether it entered his body from afar. Enraptured, he chanted these words in a sonorous voice, "Come that my eyes may not see you. Come, I have been weeping; don't resist. Come, for your own death's sake, don't be lazy. Come . . . come . . . come . . . come . . ."

The Caravanbashi and Ibrahim held their tongues and sat motionless. Suddenly, from Sayyah's side of the room, two words flew, spinning round and round, and dove into the Caravanbashi's ears.

"He's come!"

CHAPTER 17

He's Come

"He's come!"

Sayyah hung his head and took deep, agitated breaths, listening to the thumping of his own heart. When the Caravanbashi heard those two words his blood froze in his veins. Suddenly, the candle caught his eye. The candle's flame had lost its steadiness and was mischievously jumping and flickering. The smoke from the flame filled the room like mist. The Caravanbashi could hardly believe his eyes, but believe them he had to. In a single moment, the room's colour, air, and size changed.

Also at this moment, the Caravanbashi's young son, tucked up in his bed in his room in the inner quarters, rocked in the arms of a sweet sleep and had a dream that was sent for his eyes only. Inside his dream he cast a smile towards his mother who had dropped off next to him, her black hair colouring the white pillow, then this smile was coloured by the child's blood that froze in his veins.

Sensing the Caravanbashi's confusion, Sayyah sent the two words spinning and whirling their way to him again. "He's come." Then he added to those words, "Please, ask whatever you wish. He will answer you."

Ibrahim gently nudged the Caravanbashi, whispering nervously, "Master, pull yourself together. Did you hear? He's come!"

The Caravanbashi at last took himself in hand. Thinking, God willing, my wish has been granted. God help me. He carefully turned his gaze to the grey emptiness in the middle of the foggy room and in a trembling voice entreated, "Are you here, Master? Have you come? If you have come, then give me a sign."

A miracle happened. The Caravanbashi's words were hardly out of his mouth when a querulous, pitiless voice, hard as copper, sliced through the misty silence of the room and bored into the ears of all three of them. "Have you come? Haven't you come? Have you come? Haven't you come? What kind of a scoundrel are you? You've come . . . you haven't come."

His heart in his mouth from joy and fear, the Caravanbashi said, "Yes, you are here. Thank God. You're here. At last I have achieved my heart's desire."

Instinctively, he made to get up and move towards the voice, as though he wanted to touch it, but Sayyah gestured to him and he froze. He sat back down in his place. Ibrahim understood Sayyah's gesture rather differently and shuffled back as far as he could, pressing his shoulder against the cold wall.

"God be praised," a sob choked the Caravanbashi's throat. "You are here, my father, my master. Of course it's you. I knew you would come sooner or later. This is how you were in my dreams, hard and arrogant. Sir, do you know how you left me shattered, helpless? I ask you, sir. When I was old enough to understand, not a day passed, not a night, when I did not mourn, saying to myself, 'Oh, my poor father, oh, my poor brother!' Do you know this? Why are you silent? Sir, are you here?"

This time the voice of the spirit was slow to come. It was not clear whether the voice wanted to answer or not. But after a while the spirit decided to answer. When it came, the reply was unexpected. Mimicking the Caravanbashi's voice, the spirit said, "When I was old enough to understand, old enough . . . Are you always mourning? Just look at yourself!"

In his trembling heart, the Caravanbashi realised how much he yearned for that voice. The thought came to him that his father may not recognize him, for if he had recognized him he would not have spoken to him in that inexplicable way. The spirit would not be so indifferent.

He said anxiously, "God have mercy. What did you say? Why did you say that, sir? Don't you know me? I am your son, Allahverdi, sir."

This time the voice of the spirit was even more indifferent and disinterested, "You were blind and have remained blind. You are a fool. Who are you to me? What have I done that you should disturb me? Why have you summoned me here, you idiot? 'Oh my poor father, oh my poor brother, not a night passed without me saying this.' So that's how it was! What has it got to do with me? Just look at him. Look at his colour, look! You're lily white, did you know that?"

The voice of the spirit no longer came from just the middle of the room; it could be heard coming from every corner. It was a jarring, colourless voice. In one corner of the room it was a whisper, in another it was a shout, elsewhere it was furious, angry, but wherever it was, whatever form it took, the voice was still indifferent and disinterested. This was completely unexpected and confounded both the Caravanbashi and Ibrahim.

CHAPTER 18
Headsman Mammadqulu and His Son Corporal Shahveran

Wherever he might be, into whoever's face he might be looking, the Shah had in recent times taken to seeing the same mute question displayed for all to see. Those dumb looks bore the weight of longing for a new campaign, and this burden was gradually becoming unbearable. The longing for a new war, the passion for fresh plunder and pillage, filled the looks that the Shah saw every one of God's days, nay, every one of his hours. The Shah scowled; he was depressed, crushed in deep, protracted thought, wearied by his deliberations, always weighing the merits, and making decisions. Until one day, unlike the days that came before, after His Majesty had thought long and hard, he felt that he could no longer bear those cold, mute, frowning looks that insisted on new marches, and began to consider himself to blame.

"So be it!" he said. "Today is a favourable day. I have given my decision. Let the drummers play the battle drums and the standard bearers raise the battle standard before the castle!"

As soon as the news was out, triumphant shouts and a joyful mood enveloped the city. The hardened wrinkles on the faces of the servants and soldiers softened, frozen hearts began to melt, and the captains shook themselves like bears waking from their winter hibernation to ready themselves for new decrees from the Shah to prepare for the journey.

In a faraway corner of the land a beautiful city had long since revolted. Though it was not a large city, its people were renowned for their pride and dignity. The Shah's decision was aimed at bringing the city back under his control. This was a revolt that had to be crushed; the city had to answer for its actions. How often had the iron gates been barred in the faces of the Shah's emissaries? How often had insults and profanities rained down on respected persons from the town's high walls? Unwelcome words had been hurled like stones against the Shah himself.

As soon as they heard the Shah's decision, the soldiers to be sent against the mutinous city already began to act like victorious warriors. Every last resident of the capital who said half-hearted prayers to God to prolong the life of the Shah already saw them as conquerors returning victorious from the battle. Merchants, tax collectors, and land and property brokers rubbed their hands in secret, anticipating the delights of rich profits to come. They were resolved to follow hot on the heels of the troops into the defeated city.

Headsman Mammadqulu sent a man to ask his adopted son, Corporal Shahveran, to visit him that evening. He wanted to talk to him about the expedition, where it was going and why, for how long, and where the idea had come from. These questions were just one reason for the invitation. After all, he had not seen Shahveran for a long time. Shahveran's work had multiplied since his recent promotion from a rank-and-file soldier to corporal, and he rarely put in an appearance. Morning and evening, heart and soul, he was with his cohort, and often spent the night under the same roof as his troops. Before Shahveran came, Mammadqulu went early to the bazaar to buy fruit and sweetmeats, and salted a bowl of roast chickpeas. Shahveran loved roasted chickpeas.

When at last Shahveran entered the large, but ugly courtyards, his nostrils were assailed by the familiar aroma of freshly roasted chickpeas and his heart clenched as he was taken back to his childhood in these yards. He realized how much he missed his stepfather, and how he was doing Mammadqulu no good now that he was slowly growing old, when he had nothing but his work and no one with whom to share his cares. Mammadqulu was an old man, and who else did he have besides himself and an old slave. He had left him to the mercy of fate. There were days when he forgot to ask after him, let alone visit him. He had not been just a stepfather to him; he had stood in for his real father. Mammadqulu had covered him with more love than he could have given even a natural son. In return for all that, Shahveran was not doing the right thing by his stepfather, failing to repay his debt as he should.

When Shahveran of the Shahverdi family was barely two years old, Headsman Mammadqulu had despatched his father to the next world on the orders of the Shah. All his kinfolk to the seventh generation, one by one, tasted the blow of Mammadqulu's fist. Of the Shahverdi lineage, only this babe remained on the face of the earth. They had betrayed the shah, crossing the border river and planning to settle in neighbouring enemy land. What they were running from, or running to, some knew and some did not. Just as some knew that there was only one way they could run from the Shah—the way to hell, to the next world. The traitors received their punishment, their hot, steaming blood mixed with the muddy water in the narrow gutters of the charnel house. Only the babe was let free, unscathed by a sign from the enraged Shah's finger, cast aside like a discarded branch.

Turning his ashen face towards Mammadqulu, the Shah said, "Enough blood has been shed. Take him. I give him to you. You are alone and so is he. Raise him to be like you, loyal to the kingdom."

Then Mammadqulu took the babe home. He asked amongst the neighbours and found a nursemaid. The nursemaid looked after the child from morning till night. The months and years passed and Mammadqulu brought up his adopted son. Having been raised in this way, Shahveran had only boundless love and endless devotion for the Shah and Mammadqulu. Mammadqulu called him Shahveran,[10] and as the months passed he became so attached to the poor boy that he thought of him as his own son.

Now the two of them sat cross-legged at a low, round table. After talking about this and that for a good while, Mammadqulu at last came to the point and asked Shahveran, "My son, what are the soldiers saying about the expedition? Is anyone opposed to it?"

Shahveran looked in amazement at Mammadqulu, and then replied, "Sir, the expedition is an expedition like any other. There's nothing new about it. Everyone has been waiting for it for ages. Some like me are very pleased to be embarking on their first campaign. No, of course everyone is pleased. May God grant our Shah long life."

"Amen, amen. May God hear you."

Mammadqulu cast a covert look at Shahveran who was taking

---

10 The name Shahveran (Şahverən) means "gift of the Shah."

fistfuls of chickpeas, regardless of whether they were roasted or burnt, and crunching his way through them. He knew from his happy demeanour that he was looking forward to this campaign. His first military campaign, he's young and hot-blooded. He'll see new places and meet new people. God willing, how many people will fall at his feet and beg for mercy. Who knows what fate has written for him? Maybe his happiness lies in a very different place. He will follow that happiness. He will one day leave me and this place to meet his fate.

With these thoughts running through his mind, Mammadqulu could not take his eyes off the fiery youth sitting decorously before his father. His gaze kept returning to his familiar eyes and face. His moustache will be jet black, his eyes dark as pitch, his auburn hair the colour of an autumn meadow. God knows how much love I have for you in my heart, for none but you. You are my one and only love, my life, my only son, my dear.

Tucking in to the chickpeas, Shahveran sensed his stepfather's attention focused on him, but gave no sign, as his father would not want his feelings to be displayed. Mammadqulu was a secretive man, and while this secrecy led everyone around him to act with caution, Shahveran who step by step, word by word, caress by caress, had been brought up by Mammadqulu and was now a corporal with a silver-handled dagger hanging proudly from his belt, knew very well what lay behind this secrecy. As a result of this knowledge, he strove not to hinder Mammadqulu's hidden gaze. Shahveran thought to himself, Sir, you are my master. Who do I have in this world but you? And if someone appears, I don't need them, or a thousand years of riches, if I can return your hard work, repay my debt to you in this world. I have no greater desire than this—not to die before my time, so that I can serve you in your old age, take all your troubles on myself, and repay my debt to you, my father. You brought me up in place of my father, you are my one love.

Should anyone have been watching they would not have understood these two people sitting in silence opposite each other, one gazing from beneath his brows, unable to take his eyes off the other who pretended to be unaware of that gaze. They could not have understood the inner meaning of that silent conversation. Only Mammadqulu and Shahveran alone, whose hearts burned for one another, could open their hearts in this way and could comprehend each other so well. No two people could love each other as these two did, or be bound with such love. This is how their final meeting was before the campaign. There could be no other way.

CHAPTER 19
Talking to the Spirit of the Caravanbashi's Father

The Caravanbashi seemed to have frozen on the spot, lost in sorrowful thought. This was not what he had expected. He had not imagined his father's spirit being so merciless.

Ibrahim held his breath. If it had been up to him he would have put an end to the affair there and then. Enough! Did you hear? Enough! Nothing can come of this! The matter should be closed once and for all. Sayyah the Sorcerer is not the White Dervish. This is all that the spirit that he summoned can do. He should have brought the young sorcerer. He hadn't known that he was the White Dervish himself. The desire that for years had given the Caravanbashi no peace, boring a hole into his soul, was eating him up completely. If only this affair could be over quickly. Their hearts might stop otherwise.

Sayyah had shrunk so much in his corner of the room that he was hardly visible. The flickering candle flame was still sputtering. Sayyah was still sitting neatly cross-legged, his head on his chest and his hands on his knees, but had stopped rocking to and fro. He had no awareness of what was going on in the room, not even of the short, unexpected dialogue. He had secretly entered the time of solitude. Now it was impossible to pull him out and bring his being back into the room.

The Caravanbashi thought and thought and decided to try and smooth the path between him and the spirit in order to win its heart. "May I sacrifice myself for the Pivot of the Universe." The Caravanbashi turned his face to the emptiness. "Why are you so bitter? What have I done to deserve your rage?"

The spirit answered instantly, as though he had been expecting the question. "What have I done? What have I done? This is what you've done. Why have you disturbed me? Who do you think you are? What do you want from me? Why have you summoned me? That's Allahverdi. Huh! So what? It's no concern of mine!"

The spirit waited a while and then added a strange remark, "Nincompoop."

Did the Caravanbashi shudder when he heard the incomprehensible word, did the light die in his eyes? His heart leapt. Turning joyfully to Ibrahim, he looked straight at him. He opened his mouth and the words came tumbling out impatiently. "May I die at your feet. It's him, my master, it's him! May I sacrifice myself to the dust at your feet, Master, it's me. I'm Nincompoop!"

He turned slightly more towards Ibrahim. "I remember that when I was a child that is what they used to call me. When Grandma called me in, that is the name she used."

The Caravanbashi was even more convinced that the spirit in the room was the spirit of his father, Headsman Mammadqulu, and that it had definitely recognized him. Nincompoop! There couldn't be a better sign.

Re-collecting himself, the Caravanbashi tried to be patient. "Why were you talking so angrily? If you only knew how I longed for you. Sir, this longing, your sad fate, exhausts me every one of God's days!"

A sudden sobbing interrupted the Caravanbashi's words. Sorrow so filled his throat that he couldn't say another word. Silence fell. The spirit did not break the silence either. Then the Caravanbashi took himself in hand, cleared his throat, and continued to talk more easily. This time he switched to a whisper, trying to keep his voice cheerful.

"Let me make you happy, sir. You know that I have riches. I have mighty caravans. I have travelled to many countries around the world and brought curiosities back to this land." The Caravanbashi's whisper faltered, a terrible coldness penetrated his voice, "I am very close to the Shah. He likes me very much. Many people fear me. He consults me very often. You should know that this isn't the same Shah as in your day; it's his son. But what of it? He still answers for his sins. The Shah in your day, this one's father, had an ulcer, a black ulcer, and he passed away ten years ago. It was a shame he left this life so easily. I would have done it differently."

Whatever he thought, the Caravanbashi did not want to continue this subject. Casting his gaze around the room again, he began to talk in a normal voice, not a whisper. "But at night you and my brother always enter my dreams. It's true, believe me. You have me by the throat, both of you. I never saw you properly, but you don't leave my dreams, you move from one to the next. Do you know what you say to me? You don't? 'Revenge, revenge!' you say. Sometimes you whisper, and sometimes you shout, just like now. What do you want from me?"

The Caravanbashi had grown weak at the knees. He had wrenched out one of the two nails troubling his heart and hot blood was now flowing from the wound.

This time the spirit's voice had a hint of sadness as it came from near the candle. At this, the flame, which had trembled from fear, whitened. The spirit said, "Will you look at that! What is it to me who comes into and leaves your dreams, you idiot. It's not our job to go frightening anyone like a bogeyman. You couldn't sleep. I said revenge to you? I didn't! You couldn't sleep like a man. Nincompoop."

For the first time the spirit's voice wavered, but after a moment it continued with new force. "I couldn't sleep myself, but there was a reason for my sleeplessness. Do you know why I couldn't sleep? Of course you don't; how would you know, Nincompoop? Do you know who the first sacrifice was that I despatched to the next world? Do you know who breathed their last, who shed their last blood at my hand? You called me, so now you listen. But don't be afraid. It was a woman. I pushed her into a well. She died without a cry."

The Caravanbashi was so affected by this that he could scarcely stammer, "Who was it?"

The spirit continued as though he hadn't heard the question. "So . . . it was easier after that woman. It was already easy. I even enjoyed despatching one person after another to the next world on the orders of the Shah. They all went to hell of course. Did you like it? Oh, Nincompoop."

The spirit's voice was gradually becoming familiar, gradually fitting into the space. "The gossip hasn't reached you yet? Really? Is Vizier Mashdali still alive?"

After asking the last question, the spirit fell silent. But the Caravanbashi realised that this time it was a different silence; the spirit was waiting for him to answer. The Caravanbashi entreated, "Sir, why are you talking this way? Why? I'm dying. What have I done wrong, sir? Tell me what I've done wrong in your eyes! Vizier Mashdali is still alive—just. He has difficulty walking. He has to be supported on all sides or he will fall. Why did you ask about him, sir? And who was the woman you are talking about?"

The Caravanbashi screwed up his eyes, feeling horror at the answer to his question, even before he heard it. What he heard horrified him.

"Vizier Mashdali was a friend of my father's in his youth and was also my patron. It was he who covered up the death of my mother when I surrendered. I had been on the run. Yes, the identity of the woman you were asking about—she was my own mother. Had it not been for Vizier Mashdali, they would have finished me off in the mountains and fed me to the birds. What are you looking at like that? Your eyes are popping out of your head. You're funny, just like you were as a baby. Shall I tell you who the last person was I despatched to the next world? It's obvious. From a high cliff . . ."

"No, stop! Stop for a moment; have mercy. There's no hurry," the Caravanbashi moaned.

The spirit seemed to be sighing, or maybe it was just catching its breath. Cold sweat trickled down the Caravanbashi's back. Ibrahim was alarmed. He wanted to leave the room and run far away, but of course he couldn't—on pain of death, he would never leave the Caravanbashi alone in the room.

Except for candles that flickered here and there like mischievous stars, the city outside lay shrouded in darkness. Try as it might, the deep darkness could not penetrate the narrow, closed windows on the first floor of the Caravanbashi's house. The faint light of the candle protected the house's virginity like the last selfless soldier of a defeated army. The room seemed to have grown a little; the smoke-mist had found a hole in the corner and was slowly taking the life from that incomprehensible place.

Relations between the Caravanbashi and the spirit had just started to improve, but the Caravanbashi was not sure whether he could entrust his burning secrets to the spirit or not. He put his head in his hands. All the pitiless words he had heard were mixed up in his mind. The words were like camels in a caravan that could walk one after the other in single file or try to get in front, creating confusion and breaking up the line, pushing and shoving and hitting each other in fury. So what should he do now?

Ibrahim tugged at the back of the Caravanbashi's robe and whispered, "By God that's a mad spirit, sir. What do you think, light of my life, shall we drive him out? There's no good to be had from him, only evil. He is saying whatever comes into his head."

The Caravanbashi shook off Ibrahim's hand and turned to face him in the gloom, his eyes flashing so brightly that for a moment the flame of his eyes lit up the space between them. Then the Caravanbashi turned back, the flame in his eyes extinguished. The darkness spread to every corner of the room, crossing the boundary of the flickering candle light. The Caravanbashi looked towards the spot where the spirit's voice had last been heard near the candle and waited to see what it would say next.

"First of all, there's something you should know," the spirit continued calmly. 'If I don't tell you, someone else will. It was me, no one else, me who sent her to the next world face down from the top of the mountain. She wanted to fly, but had no wings. Where would she have flown? She couldn't fly; she plummeted like a stone to the bottom of the valley. She twitched and then moved no more."

This time the Caravanbashi whispered a soft entreaty as though to himself, "No . . ."

The bitter spirit did not hear him. "That was my last execution. The first was my mother, the last your mother. You say you went blind from weeping and you see me every night in your dreams. What about your mother? Don't you see her? Oh, Nincompoop."

The Caravanbashi spoke very softly again, "Sir, this is killing me. Don't talk like that. Have mercy on me."

He turned back to face Ibrahim. "What is he saying? Do you understand anything? Maybe this isn't my father at all? Oh God, who is this?"

Ibrahim could bear it no longer. Without further ado, he got up, his hands clutched to his chest as though to keep in his anxiety, and feeling his way along the wall went to Sayyah. Sayyah did not change his position, but opened his eyes a crack and looked at him with amazement as though to say, "What is it? What do you want?" Ibrahim fell to his knees before him, begging, "For the love of God, tell me who this is. Whose spirit is this?"

A faint light of surprise filled Sayyah's half-closed eyes. "It is the spirit of your master, the Caravanbashi's father. Whose spirit could it be? There can be no doubt. It's Headsman Mammadqulu's spirit."

"Are you sure?"

"Of course I'm sure. What of it?"

Ibrahim stared hard at Sayyah's slowly closing eyes for a moment, as though he wanted to test whether what he had said was right or not. Then without giving an answer he returned to his place the same way he had come, feeling his way along the wall, and sat down cross-legged again.

Leaning towards the Caravanbashi, he whispered, "It's him, light of my eyes, your father. Be strong and bear it. What else can we do?"

This time the spirit spoke with a hint of kindness. "How you've grown! You were a scrap of a lad. Your old grandmother used to sing you a lullaby . . ."

> Sleep, baby, sleep,
> If you don't sleep,

If you don't dream,
If you cry and scream,
The Bogeyman will come and get you.

"Oh, Nincompoop . . ." The spirit's voice was already weak. "I'm your master. Who am I? I'm your father, your wretched father."

The Caravanbashi nearly fainted at the spirit's latest words. Several incidents from his childhood, half-shrouded in mist, swam before his eyes. Familiar distant voices rang in his ears, "The Bogeyman . . . will come and get you."

"When I grew up, I feared no bogeymen in this world." The Caravanbashi sank in an ocean of sadness. "The Bogeyman . . . However much I asked my old grandma, she never said who the Bogeyman was, where he came from, or where he was going. She would just moan 'revenge, revenge.' Can you hear me, sir? Are you making fun of me? Tell me you were lying; I don't believe it."

The spirit replied bitterly, "We cannot lie. Even if I want to, I cannot." Then the spirit raised his voice again, "If you've nothing else to say, then I'm off. Oh, Nincompoop, have you anything to say?"

This time the Caravanbashi almost begged the spirit, "Stay awhile. God, don't be in a hurry. Tell me, have you seen my brother there, my young innocent brother drenched in blood?"

The spirit bristled, "I don't know what you're talking about. I don't know him, do you understand? I don't know him. Over there I forget what happened here. Our memories wake up when we come back here. I've forgotten him. It's better that way. It's as though everyone is my son. I don't know my own father either. It's as though everyone is my father. And he doesn't know me. I'm going. It's pointless. Pointless! I've no interest in pointless conversation, and you're making me uncomfortable. Don't go summoning me here again, do you hear me?"

The spirit's voice faded again. Words were a jumble of shouts and whispers, so it was impossible to make out anything in the din. But in a short while the voice regained its previous harshness, and the spirit continued to speak in a measured way, "Do you know why they drenched your brother in blood? You don't, do you? They did it because of you! You had come into the world. After that I was bound even more closely to that house, to that hearth, to that city. I wanted to stay with your mother. I committed a true sin. I disobeyed the Shah's order. I should have left with the troops, but I didn't; I stayed. That was my sin. They vented their wrath on us. Your mother paid for that sin too, you know."

The Caravanbashi asked in surprise, "They took it out on me, a mere babe?"

The spirit swiftly confirmed this, "Yes, on you! They took revenge on me and on him for you coming into this world. I arrived in your mother's city with the army, and I should have left with the army too. But . . . I didn't leave. I loved your mother, you see. I disregarded the Shah's order. That is a sin! The decree of the Shah was read out to the troops on every street corner. The decree said that whoever set out with me and my army and travelled this far must return to the capital with me, let him not dare to remain. Should anyone intend to remain in this defeated land, his entire lineage would be wiped out, as everything in this defeated land, the air, the water, the earth, the rocks, the grain and bread, had already been castrated. That was the decree. One night they threw a sack in front of my house. It contained Shahveran's severed head."

CHAPTER 20

The Shah's Revenge

Then ight was jet black, the sky starless. Wherever the stars had disappeared to, their lofty positions in the heavens now seemed a half-forgotten dream on some distant night. The spirit of the stars had been wiped from the watchers down below. A black cloud had again moved in front of the white-faced moon, angrily extinguishing its light, and a deep shadow descended on the beautiful Parnisa's yard.

Mammadqulu was lying in his bed, one hand in the sweetly sleeping Parnisa's tousled hair, the other . . . when suddenly he heard the sound of horseshoes striking the cobbles like hammers. The sound came closer and closer until it reached the gate to the yard. It then stopped abruptly and silence fell. Mammadqulu propped himself up on the pillows, his heart gripped by a sense of foreboding. With his eyes as well as his ears, he searched for the source of the noise that had stopped so suddenly, but could find nothing. That's when Mammadqulu's anxious heart really started to pound. It pounded and pounded until he heard a man's voice outside.

Whoever it was was slowly climbing the ladder, and whispered through the open window, "Traitor Mammadqulu, take the answer to your treachery. This is your answer—take it." Then something hit the ground with a thud, as though the men down below at the gate had spoken. The clattering of hooves rose up as the horses turned around and galloped off the way they had come, their shoes beating a wild rhythm through the streets. The sounds grew ever more distant until silence fell again. No sound was to be heard.

Mammadqulu was frozen to the spot, leaning on the pillows. He didn't dare move even a single hair. He had turned into a statue. He hardly dared breathe, lest the movement disturb Parnisa. I mustn't move, I mustn't make a sound. The moment had its secret and it lay in keeping stock still. A good while passed in this way. The silence had turned into a shrill, piercing cry when someone seemed to have nudged Parnisa, waking her up. Why are you sleeping? Open your eyes, look, see how he has turned into a statue next to you, how his body, his face, his eyes have shrunk, how he's aged. The moment Mammadqulu's eyes rested on Parnisa, he seemed to take courage from his befuddled state, rose slowly from the bed, and began to get dressed.

Parnisa hugged herself from fear. "What's wrong? Where are you going?" she whispered.

Mammadqulu did not answer, but gave her a very strange look. As he sadly climbed down the ladder towards the gate, a smile flew from the distant past and settled on his lips like a dove. The secret of the moment seemed to have flown away. Then it was that Mammadqulu understood what had happened. He realized what was in that sack that had thudded to the ground. The smile like a dove on his lips, he slid the bolt back and opened the iron gates. When he went out into the silent, empty street, he saw a large black sack that had been thrown at the gate. As he dragged the sack into the yard, it left a black trail behind. The stench from the trail was a familiar one to Mammadqulu. He knew it so well. He clenched his lips and for the first time in his life felt his knees go weak. He shook like a tall tower in an earthquake, and as soon as he was in the yard fell to his knees beside the sack, clutched at his face with his hands, and from his heart cried only these two words, "Shahveran, no . . ."

Mammadqulu and his old retainer took Shahveran's body to a green valley outside the city where a spring babbled unknown to the world at the foot of sheer cliffs. This is where they consigned his body to the earth. As he dug the grave, as he placed Shahveran's body in it, as he covered him with earth, he felt as though he had dug his own grave, put himself in it, and covered himself with dirt. It seemed to him that another Mammadqulu came face to face with the hand that emerged from his body and, trying to hold the air with this hand, he placed himself into the same grave.

The old slave, who had seen the world, sat to one side, staring silently into the distance. He kept his gaze averted, as he could not look Mammadqulu in the face. But suddenly he glanced towards him and saw a gentle smile settle on Mammadqulu's lips, and his master almost laughed as he squatted at the graveside.

The old slave barked out, "May God have mercy! God is great!" He then cleared his throat and began to cough very loudly. He coughed twice, but the smile that had turned into a dove stayed on Mammadqulu's lips. It did not fly away.

Chapter 21
Continuing the Conversation with the Spirit

A n eerie silence settled in the room. It was the spirit that broke it. "Do not ask me again about Shahveran. Do you hear? Don't ask me again. You know all about yourself, you won't hear anything more from me."

Ibrahim gave the Caravanbashi another gentle nudge from behind. "Master, finish this conversation. For God's sake, you cannot know but you have no colour in your face, no light in your eyes. What more do you have to do with this mad spirit's ridiculous remarks?"

The Caravanbashi turned and gave Ibrahim such a look that he fell silent. "No, you don't know; that's not how it is. Do this. Go outside; I have something to ask him alone."

The frightened Ibrahim tried to speak, "Light of my eyes—"

"Enough!" The Caravanbashi interrupted him angrily. Then he reconsidered and said more calmly, "Leave the room please; give me a moment alone with him. I have something to say."

Though he was offended, Ibrahim agreed this time. "Very well, what can I say? You tell me to go outside, so I will. But I'll be close by, light of my life. I won't go far. If anything happens, call me." Without further ado, he crawled out of the room.

First, the Caravanbashi let his eyes roam the room. He

thought that if he could hear the voice of the spirit then maybe he could see him too. Where was he? Was there really no trace of him?

Without waiting for a question, the spirit began to speak. "You have asked whatever you wanted to and more. I am aware of your circumstances—you have wealth, property, you can talk to the Shah. What more do you need? Let me go."

Whoever had summoned the spirit gave permission for him to leave, and that was Sayyah the Sorcerer. Only he could return the spirit to his own place. But the Caravanbashi had not heard the spirit's last request; he was lost in his own thoughts. He thought the time had come to reveal what he had kept secret in his heart. He said in a rush, "Sir, I will avenge you both."

The spirit was amazed. "Avenge us, boy? On whom take vengeance? What are you talking about?"

"I will, of course I will. I have said so." At last the Caravanbashi felt peace in his heart. The nail he had driven into his heart many years ago was no more. It had been pulled out and dissolved like sugar.

"I have said so," he repeated stubbornly.

"No, you're not making sense. Look at it more closely." The spirit had not expected this turn in the conversation at all.

The Caravanbashi had not believed that the long-awaited time would come when he would be free of the pain he had carried in his heart for so many years. Those words that he had collected in his heart year by year, month by month, day by day, hour by hour, he had spoken in one moment to their intended recipient. But this was not happiness; happiness was for the Caravanbashi to see himself from the side.

He looked and saw an agitated young man sitting cross-legged in a familiar room. The young man turned and said something in an unfamiliar voice. He spoke into the emptiness as though someone was listening in this murky room that had now lost its familiar contours. The Caravanbashi knew and yet did not know this young man. There was a resemblance to someone. The young man was saying something, trying hard to prove something, but the Caravanbashi was no longer listening. He didn't want to listen to anything; he just wanted to be lost in loving contemplation of him, but the words found their way in this impenetrable, penetrable mist.

"Ever since I left childhood I have lived with the word vengeance. At night I fell asleep with the word vengeance on my lips, and in the morning when I awoke it fell like dried mud from my lips into the next evening's embrace. What do you want to tell me now? Every God-given day my old grandmother put this word in my ears like an earring. When she was dying and had lost the power of speech, her eyes said 'Vengeance!' She also told me this with her eyes, 'If you forget vengeance for a moment, my brave boy, if you forget, the Bogeyman . . .' I quickly said, 'No, I won't forget; you can breathe easy, I won't forget.' Her eyes said again, 'If you do, then. . .' I said, 'If I forget, may the Bogeyman come and get me.'

"At first I did not forget this word out of fear. It was a word. Just as I do not forget to breathe the air, I did not forget. Just as I do not forget to eat bread, I did not forget. Just as I do not forget to quench my thirst with water . . . But you . . ."

CHAPTER 22
Jt Js for God to Punish, Don't Meddle ın God's Affaırs!

The Caravanbashi paused for breath. He forgot where he was, who he was talking to, closed his eyes, and fell into the warm embrace of memory, which whisked him away to the distant years of childhood.

His old grandmother was still alive, but only just. She lay on her bed, shrunken in her wooden body, no life force left, struggling to breathe, struggling to talk. She was skin and bones, only her eyes shone with light.

"You know your father left a golden pitcher." Licking her parched lips to moisten them, his grandmother talked more with her eyes than her tongue. "This is the first time I have uttered these words. Listen and don't forget. I brought you up half-starved, half-full, but did not touch the gold, did not uncork the pitcher. Now my time has come and I must tell you the secret. Death is at my threshold. I will not take the gold to my grave; you may need it here. In the yard, in the upper wall of the well . .

. there is a hollow. The pitcher is inside that hollow. It is covered with twigs and brushwood; the birds have built a nest there now. Look, your father Mammadqulu's gold is there. The murderer of your father and brother . . ."

In the flashes of bright light behind his closed eyes, the Caravanbashi saw the small child struggle to overcome his fear, saw him lean taut as a bow over his scarcely breathing grandmother and whisper to her unblinking eyes, "Who? Who is their murderer? Don't die, Grandma, don't go yet."

Smiling with her eyes, the old grandmother croaked, "Ah, give me a moment. Don't be afraid, I won't die until you say it."

"Who was it? You always said, 'Wait, the time will come and I'll tell you.' That it's me who must seek vengeance."

"I know, my little lamb, I know. Let me tell you. Your father was amongst the troops that entered our city. He was the headsman. He was a trusted servant of the Shah. He stayed in the house next to ours. His window looked down into our yard. That window isn't there anymore. Your father bricked it up. Help me sit up; I can't breathe. Oh God, help me."

With both hands, the small child reached behind his grandmother's neck and pulled her up on her mattress. Then, with one hand he held her neck and adjusted her pillow with the other. Only then could the old woman breathe properly.

"Your father and my daughter, Parnisa," the old grandmother forced herself to go on, "oh God, I get so angry when I think of it; my daughter fell in love with him. He drooled as he watched her from the window . . . in the moonlight . . . and she sat at the door, gazing up tenderly at him. They forgot their honour, both of them. They used to wait for the moon to disappear, and the yard to be in darkness. I pretended to be asleep. What could I do? She was a poor young widow. How could I protect her from a buffalo in heat? Do you know what nonsense my own daughter told me? Oh . . ."

The old grandmother stopped to get her breath. Another memory had taken her far away. Then suddenly she remembered something and sat bolt upright, supporting herself with her hands. She amazed herself as the dark cry came from her breast to her lips, from her lips to the light of the world, "What hell are you in, my daughter Parnisa? What, haven't you finished hanging out that washing yet? Was it such a big job? Come inside, go to bed, it's late, I'm falling asleep. Parnisa, you shameless hussy . . ."

The old grandmother screeched those words and then fell silent. Her head fell back on the pillow and she lost consciousness.

The Caravanbashi's eyes were closed. From those closed eyes tears started to flow. They poured down his face into his beard and then fell onto the carpet.

The old grandmother slowly came to, gave a groan from deep inside her, and searched for the child with her eyes. When she found him, she said, "Every night, a wisp of cloud would cover that bright moon. Give me your hand . . ."

The old grandmother held tightly to the child's hand and hurried to continue. "At this time the whole yard would be plunged in darkness. Your mother . . . every night when I had gone to bed your mother would climb the ladder to your father's window and scramble inside. Sometimes I slept, but sometimes I did not. She paid no attention."

The small child was listening but the words went in one ear and out through the other. They did not lodge themselves in his mind. He was waiting for just one word. He was waiting for his old grandmother to say who had killed his father and brother. When he heard the name, it would be engraved on his heart, and step by step, day by day, breath by breath he would pursue his victim and wreak vengeance.

The old grandmother's breathing was ragged. Her eyes widened and she looked intently around her, as though she was seeing the world for the first time. In this state, she spoke her last words very clearly and slowly, and at ease finally breathed her last.

"Your enemy, my child, is a powerful enemy, a great enemy. You will need this gold. Your father's murderer—don't forget, my child, don't forget a thing, your father's murderer was the Shah himself."

The old grandmother spoke those words in a single breath, then let go of the child's hand. Her breath did not return; her open eyes were still.

At these words, two spots burned on the child's cheeks as he bent over his grandmother. He took his her hand from the floor and placed it on her dried chest. He drew back a little, looked intently into his old grandmother's face, and then hurried out of the room. He travelled a long road until at last he entered the room where the Caravanbashi was now sitting and looked until he found him. When he entered the room, he was no longer a child; he was already the Caravanbashi himself. The two merged into one.

The spirit's voice shook the Caravanbashi from his thoughts, "Are you listening to me? I am very tired. You look tired too. Many things should now be clear to you. Is your heart easier now?"

The Caravanbashi parroted stubbornly, "I will avenge you. Say what you like, I will avenge you. Say what you like, but I will do it!"

Bitter laughter entered the spirit's troubled voice, "On whom will you take vengeance, Nincompoop? You keep saying 'my brother, my brother,' but you know he wasn't your real brother."

The Caravanbashi ignored this. "Didn't you avenge your father? Yes, you did."

"And as a result, my whole life was empty," the spirit said bitterly. "If you pledge vengeance you won't be able to live. You will not have the strength to live."

The Caravanbashi remembered his old grandmother's glittering inheritance. "When my old grandmother died, she gave me a pitcher of gold and told me it was my inheritance. She said my father left it. She said my enemy was a great enemy, a powerful one. 'Add to this gold, don't let it shrink,' she said. She said I could have vengeance only through the might of this gold."

The spirit hissed venomously, "Oh, that witch and her pitcher!"

"She brought me up, sir; don't forget that. She did not betray that trust. Don't talk like that about her."

"She did not like me at all." The spirit's voice became animated as he revisited the past. "All that time, we didn't exchange two words. She always treated me like a heathen. But it seems that she was loyal."

"You were saying that the gold—"

"Yes," the spirit interrupted. "Yes, of course, it wasn't yours!"

"Then whose was it?" The Caravanbashi was astounded.

"The Shah's."

"The Shah's?"

The Caravanbashi was amazed. The main purpose of his life melted before his eyes like a snowball in the heat of summer. He could only stammer, "No sir, don't talk like that. I beg you, don't say that. You said the Shah was my greatest enemy."

"Look," the spirit's voice grew louder. "He's my greatest enemy, you say. Why? Or . . ."

"Yes sir, because of you, because of my brother."

"What did you say, boy?"

"Yes sir, I know what you're going to say. You're right that it wasn't this Shah that oppressed you, it was his grandfather, but I cannot leave your blood unavenged. I will take vengeance on his son. I will not leave my brother's blood on the ground. I will not. How many nights I groaned my brother's name, my poor brother whose life was snatched from him." The Caravanbashi's voice choked with tears.

As the wind howled through the solitary window, the candle flame flickered and almost went out. The Caravanbashi rubbed his eyes roughly with the backs of his hands, pushing the tears back. Remembering what the spirit had said about his brother a few moments ago, he added, "You can't say anything to stop me loving my brother, sir."

"How will you exact your vengeance, you wretch?" the spirit asked hopelessly, interrupting him.

The Caravanbashi looked again to all four corners of the room, training his gaze on Sayyah who remained motionless, his eyes closed. He was sure that apart from himself and Sayyah there was no other living creature in the room. Sayyah was lost in his own rapture and could not hear them; maybe he had entered his time of solitude. Nevertheless, the Caravanbashi carefully cast his gaze around the room again, making sure that only his father, this strange spirit, would hear what he had to say. He cleared his throat and quietly, but firmly, revealed what was in his heart.

"I will have it. You know, sir, I am one of his most trusted men. I am his first merchant. Whatever his wife and children order, I get it. I will poison him. He will die slowly. He will die a dog's painful death. No one will be able to comprehend whose work it was. So what if he is the Shah! He should pay for his father's deeds."

The Caravanbashi was silent. He wiped the sweat from the back of his neck with a silk cloth. In a moment, the cloth was soaked and he threw it aside behind the bolster. "Now what do you have to say?" he asked, hoping for approval.

This time the spirit's voice was full of sorrow. It cut to the heart. "You were a baby, a tiny child. You were so lovely as you sucked your mother's small white breasts. Nincompoop, don't do this."

The Caravanbashi was bewildered. This was the last answer he had expected from his father. He said softly and urgently, "No one will know. I will give him an ancient staff. In the land of the heathens there is a city in the sea. I brought it back from there myself."

The Caravanbashi could not bear the tension. Interrupting himself, he rose and moved towards the door. "Let's see if that wretch is eavesdropping!"

He pressed his ear to the door. No, there's not a soul there, he thought to himself and then suddenly flung the door open. There really wasn't a soul there. He closed the door, went back to his place, and sat down cross-legged again.

"No, there's no one there. It's quiet. No one is eavesdropping. In short, I can tell you that inside that staff is a long glass vessel full of holes. It has been filled with poison. Every time the staff is put down, poison will be released and mix with the air inside his lungs. He seized it as soon as he saw it. He really was touched by the evil eye. It is a truly beautiful piece of handiwork. You cannot take your eyes off it.

"He has a limp, you know. When he was a child he had a dog, a puppy, and it fell into a pool of water. He jumped in to rescue it and hurt his leg, and ever since he has walked with a limp. Yes sir, I have carefully thought this through. I will achieve my goal."

"But why?" asked the spirit. "Have you really thought why? The Shah's father is dead. What fault is it of his? And how do you know this will be a blessing for me? You haven't thought whether it is better for me to be here with you or there? What vengeance will you seek for me? Do I need this? It's pointless, my child, pointless."

The spirit fell into a hopeless silence, while the Caravanbashi rushed to object. "No, it's not pointless!" he said, raising his voice. "This is in return for our suffering. This world has its own reckoning. Maybe over there you've all lost your senses. Maybe you've forgotten everything, but we do not forget anything. His sin is great—of course it is!"

"You're talking fairy tales. Everyone is a sinner. Who is without sin? Did what happened to me happen for no reason? No. Did I disobey my benefactor? I did. I deserved to receive my punishment and I received it. Just think about it."

"What should I think about? What about my brother?"

"There you go, saying 'my brother' again. Sin was committed, my child. My sin, your sin, his sin, what difference does it make? Sin was committed. Don't do this."

The Caravanbashi felt the spirit's voice in his hair, as though he were gently stroking it. He whispered, "Sir, I would sacrifice myself for you. Give me your blessing."

"Listen carefully to me, my child, listen carefully. You must continue our lineage; you must live. Do you know," the spirit prepared to make a sad confession, "do you know how beautiful this life is? Remove this flame of vengeance from your heart, extinguish it and reduce it to ashes. You say you have everything—goods, riches, luxury—but where is your peace of mind, my child? You have no peace. I pity you."

"If I do not do this, I shall never have a moment's peace. All my life I have had no peace. I don't know what it is to rest."

"And if you manage to do this, you will find rest?"

"I will."

"You won't. You cannot punish another, boy. It is for God to punish! He will give to each what they deserve. Do not interfere in God's work, my child."

The Caravanbashi did not respond. His head dropped to his chest and his heart pounded. Suddenly he understood the difficulty of the task he had undertaken. He sighed. He realized it was high time to end the conversation because the deed was already done, the arrow had been shot.

Tired, he confessed, "You know, sir, I have already given that staff to the Shah. The die has been cast. Do you know how pleased he was when he took the it? It was such a beautiful staff."

"Nincompoop, Nincompoop . . . What have you done? Does a slave of God raise his hand against God's shadow on this earth? You're no slave of God."

"No sir, I am acting justly." Though he was exhausted, the Caravanbashi stuck to his position like a blind man summoning the last of his strength.

The spirit was silent while he got his breath back. Seeming to be debating with himself, he suddenly said, "You are no child of mine if you do not fall to your knees before the Shah and seek his forgiveness. Tell him everything—beg, plead, shed tears. I know them well. Tell him everything yourself and he might forgive your sin—maybe."

The Caravanbashi smiled bitterly. "It's too late, sir."

This time the spirit muttering to itself. Straining to hear what it was saying, the Caravanbashi made out, "My child, if they had given her to me, that old grandmother, my black slave and I would have poured molten lead down her throat. How beautifully I would have stitched up her tongue that kept telling you to seek vengeance. The old witch!"

For the first time since his contact with the spirit, a gentle joy filled the Caravanbashi's heart like a delicate butterfly settling on a leaf. "Sir, I sacrifice myself to your tongue; I sacrifice myself to your words. Are you so fired up on my behalf? Oh God, I am so happy. If only you knew how happy you have made me, sir!"

The spirit was silent. All that could be heard was the whistling of the blizzard outside. The delicate butterfly that had settled on the Caravanbashi's heart trembled at the sound of the storm and flew away. Dark thoughts returned to him and he asked, "Sir, so I have lived my life in vain all these years?" The Caravanbashi's words were mixed with bitter tears that he was unaware of.

"Don't cry like a girl," the spirit said severely. "Get up and go to the palace. Hurry up and tell him the secret of the staff before anyone else does. Do as I have said."

"No, I can't. I've no strength left. I can't even get up from the floor."

At this point in the conversation, a noise was heard out in the street. Suddenly there was a loud banging at the gate to the yard. It was a band of the Shah's forces. Ten to fifteen men stood at the gate, their swords drawn. Some struck the iron gates with stones. They were the Shah's special punitive detachment. The commotion woke the servants sleeping in the house at the far side of the yard. It woke the serving maids on the top floor of the house, and the Caravanbashi's wife and child, setting them all into a panic. No one knew what to do. Some scurried back and forth ineffectually, others curled up in corners.

Deeply agitated, Ibrahim rushed to the Caravanbashi's room. "Light of my eyes, soldiers have come from the Shah! Do you hear? They are breaking down the gate! They say the Shah is summoning you—now, at this hour. He told the soldiers to fetch you. They are not saying what's happened. Do you know anything?"

The Caravanbashi did not know where the strength in his legs came from. He leapt to his feet and said decisively, "Soldiers are here, you say? Go and tell them I'm coming. They don't need to make such a noise. Tell them I'll come as soon as I've finished my ablutions. Go on!"

Ibrahim swallowed the word that was on his tongue, turned, and went out into the yard. He went up to the gate, which was shaking from the blows, and shouted over the wall, "He's coming, he's coming! Have some patience! He's performing his ablutions and will come as soon as he's finished." The clamour in the street subsided. The punitive detachment decided to wait.

The Caravanbashi went up to the window in the middle of the room and looked out. "Sir, can you show yourself to me?" he asked.

"No, I can't. We're not able to do that," the spirit answered sadly.

"This is our last meeting, sir. I have a request."

"Tell me."

"Sir, all my life I have longed for you. I did not remember my mother, my own mother, even once, only you and my brother. But now, you see, I have remembered my mother." The Caravanbashi fell silent. Opening his arms, he raised them to the sky and gave a groan from the very bottom of his heart. "Tell me about my mother, sir. Tell me what happened."

Sayyah rose slowly from the place where he had been sitting so quietly, walked past the Caravanbashi, whose arms remained outstretched, and left the room.

CHAPTER 23

Beautiful Parnisa Is No More

A while later, the troops led by the Shah left this defeated city, its previous waywardness beaten out of it. The unfortunate, stubborn Mammadqulu had not abandoned his decision and was the only person from the troops to stay behind in the city. He had already made Parnisa his wife and she had borne him a son. Mammadqulu thought long and hard and decided to call his son Allahverdi,[11] but now and again he teased him affectionately, calling him Nincompoop.

One long night after Shahveran, Mammadqulu could not sleep, try as he might. Eventually, he gently nudged the Parnisa, who was fast asleep at his side, stroked her golden hair and whispered, "Don't be afraid, get up. It's time."

At first, Parnisa didn't understand and thought her baby was crying to be fed. Then she remembered that the child was sleeping with her old mother that night. Without saying a word, she got up. Without looking at one another, they slowly got dressed. When she was dressed, Parnisa stood facing Mammadqulu.

He gazed, captivated, at his wife, his eyes full of grief. A groan erupted from deep within his breast, and then he hung his head again. "Let's go," he whispered.

---

11 The name Allahverdi means 'given by God', equivalent to the name Theodore.

139

The two of them climbed down the ladder, Mammadqulu in front. They opened the gate carefully so as not to make a sound, and went out into the street, Mammadqulu in front again. They walked a short way from the city until they reached a familiar spot, a cliff, and walked to the top. Below lay a deep gorge. Water from a spring snaked playfully around their feet, then found a suitable spot to throw itself like a pining lover into the leafy embrace of the gorge. It wound wearily round the new grave at the foot of the gorge before continuing on its way. The pair found a suitable spot and sat down, back to back. They were pressed up so close to each other that anyone looking from a distance would have seen one body, not two.

That motionless, fearless body held the two trembling souls tight within it and did not want to let them go. Parnisa felt the green grass with her hand. She chose a long blade, plucked it, put it in her mouth, and began to chew. They sat a while in silence, the only sound the babbling of the spring. "God help us," Mammadqulu said and rose.

Parnisa, who had been his support behind, put her hands on the ground and got up, saying, "God help us." But she did not turn round to face Mammadqulu and stood with her back towards him.

She chewed the grass more intensely, its bitterness flooding her tongue, her mouth, her brain, but she did not stop chewing. Mammadqulu lost no more time. He took a deep breath and, with one hand her waist and the other at her feet, swung her now solitary young body up above his head. At this moment he looked up at the sky and saw salt crystals scattered across the heavens, salt crystals commonly known as stars gathered together or standing in rows or on their own. The thought flashed through his mind that it would be hot tomorrow, how the child would wake up the next morning bound to his grandmother's crooked back, and waving his arms out of his swaddling clothes would yell at the top of his voice. And his old grandmother would pretend to be deaf and pay no attention to his cries, humming the lullaby.

Sleep, bonny baby, sleep.
Stretch out a carpet in the shade of the elm,
And I'll tell you the tales of the hidden night stars.
If you don't sleep,
The Bogeyman will come and get you.

Strange as it may seem, he knew the child would drift off to sleep to the rhythm of that voice and a morning unlike any that had gone before would begin.

But what was her sin after all? She had none. What if this poor wretch was the cause of the calamity that had befallen him? So many other causes could be found. No, I've changed my mind, I will not do this, thought Mammadqulu, wanting to put Parnisa back down on the ground and stroke her silken hair again with his calloused fingers, so that the trembling girl snuggled up against him and they, who had come as two people, could return home to the city as one. Suddenly he realized that his outstretched hands no longer bore any weight. Who would he put back on the ground? A moment ago Parnisa had been in his hands, but now they were empty. Like two drawn swords, they were trained on the heavens. Were they threatening the stars? They were. Parnisa had uttered no plea, no complaint, and no reproach. She was no more. Then where was she, God's poor slave? Why did Mammadqulu keep his empty hands raised to the sky? How long did he keep his hands stretched out to the stars? He wanted to drop his hands to his sides, but couldn't.

A vision appeared before his eyes. After he had pushed his mother down the well, he ran agitated into the yard of Zabulla the Merchant, who at midnight was fast asleep under the elm. When he plunged his dagger into the top of his heart, a delicate bird came from nowhere and settled on Zabulla's lips. That smile remained on his lips as he died. Mammadqulu was amazed that he died smiling. Why had his hands turned to stone? Why were they outstretched, motionless, like two bird's wings—no, like two drawn swords—trained on the heavens?

At last Mammadqulu wrenched his gaze away from his petrified hands and, looking again at the omniscient stars winking slyly at him from the heavens, he saw that they had begun to age; they were slowly shrinking, dissolving, and trickling down. They were no longer there really, or they were behind a tulle curtain as morning struggled to come. But where had the girl gone? What had happened to her? Was Mammadqulu, whose shoulders heaved with silent sobs and whose eyes shed lively tears, amazed at this? He was.

Chapter 24
The Killing of the Caravanbashi

The Caravanbashi stood silently in the middle of the room, his hands still raised to the heavens. He slowly came to. After a while he let his arms fall hopelessly to his sides and returned to his old place, sitting back down cross-legged. But he did not seek out the spirit in the room with either with his eyes or ears, and said quietly, as though to himself, "Sir, you know death is a good thing if you do not sense its approach. Many times, on those distant nights as I rocked on a camel's back, I tried to picture my death but could not."

The spirit said, "My child, I'm telling you, don't stay here any longer. I know what awaits you. Run, get out. Go and save your life wherever your eyes turn or your feet take you."

Without knocking for permission, the alarmed Ibrahim entered the room. "Light of my life, I went and told the soldiers that you're coming, but they are impatient. They say that if you don't come out, they will break down the gates and put us all to the sword, women and children. They say the Shah is raging against you. They say you tried to poison him."

"Go back to them and beg them; tell them I'm coming. Where would I run to? Go back to them. No, stop!" The Caravanbashi took a breath. 'I entrust my only son to you. Don't forget that I saved your life."

"I will not forget, light of my life!" Khaja Ibrahim said, tears pouring unbidden from his eyes. "I will never forget!"

In his heart he thought, Sayyah the Sorcerer was right when he said as we crossed the plain that you have a different kind of love. If something happens to him, how will I live?

The spirit exclaimed again, "That old witch! That old crone! She got what she wanted. She's taken her revenge on me."

The Caravanbashi paid no attention to the voice. Taking Ibrahim's hand, he begged, "See, Ibrahim, my end has come. You will stay; you know all my secrets, you know where my gold is. Take it, do whatever you like with it, but look after my son. Go now, they've started to make a noise again."

Ibrahim hugged the Caravanbashi tightly then quickly let him go. With a great sob he left the room, tears in his eyes.

This time the voices coming from the street were angrier, more threatening. They were no longer knocking at the gate, they were breaking it down. One of the soldiers picked up a huge stone from the ground and, summoning all his strength, hurled it over the wall. The stone flew into the yard and fell at Ibrahim's feet as he ran breathlessly from the house. He whispered, "May God have mercy," then turned towards the gate, shouting, "Can't you show some patience? What is this? Wait a couple of minutes! He's coming!"

The wife and child had already got up and come out into the yard. The Caravanbashi's small son was trembling and hanging on to the edge of his mother's dress. With one hand his bewildered mother was pressing him to her stomach, and with the other trying to push her unruly hair under her shawl.

In the half-light of early morning, the occasional snowflake flew across the sky, the defeated remnants of last night's snow that cast a white shawl over the high elms planted along the wall. The flakes fluttered across the yard, soft bright particles of light in the dark, freezing air.

Sayyah came out into the yard, a prayer mat and a bundle in his hands. The spirit and the Caravanbashi were left alone together. Suddenly the window in their room that looked out onto the yard was flung open. The Caravanbashi appeared in the window and shouted with all his strength in the direction of the gate that was now almost off its hinges under the rhythmic blows. "God is great! I said I'm coming. Can't you be patient just for a moment? I'm coming!"

The sound of blows against the gate subsided. But one soldier could not calm down and his fur hat appeared above the gate as he tried to climb over. From the top of the wall he looked wildly around the yard. At first he could see no one, as the servants cowered silently in their quarters. Then he made out Khaja Ibrahim at the gate, then the mother and child close to the door of the house, and then Sayyah the Sorcerer. Try as he might, that soldier staring greedily into the yard saw no one else.

The Caravanbashi clicked the window shut and was about to leave the room when he hesitated. Turning to the emptiness he said, "I'm going, sir. You said that I would not know you or my brother over there, didn't you?"

"I did," the spirit replied.

"Are you still here?"

"I'm here!" The spirit was still in the room. The flame of the candle in the candlestick on the low table in the middle of the room was still flickering, and though it was a broken wave of light, the candle still spread warmth.

"So we shall never meet again. Unless Fate wills, who

knows? No one knows. Wait, don't leave me alone."

Though the spirit's answer froze the blood in his veins, the Caravanbashi gave no sign of his consternation. "Do you know what you should do? Take the dagger hanging from this carpet. Take it, don't hold back, and don't let your hands shake. This is very easy. Don't give yourself into the Shah's hands. The torture will be great. Plunge it into the top of your heart, as if you were putting something back in its place."

Without thinking of anything else, as though he had long been expecting these words, the Caravanbashi seized the dagger hanging from the carpet on the wall and drew it from its scabbard. He stared in surprise at the blade, dazzled as it gleamed in the half-light of the room. He blinked hard and, without saying a word, thrust the sharp-tipped blade into his breast, right up to the hilt. The dagger cut his heart in two. From the rupture in his heart two drops of blood flowed up through his throat and rested on his lips. His last words wrenched from his soul mixed with those two drops of blood.

"Farewell, Father."

The Caravanbashi did not hear the spirit's last words. "Farewell, my son!"

CHAPTER 25

Sayyah the Sorcerer, the Caravanbashi's Son, and the City Lost in the Snow

The soldiers at last forced the gate open and poured into the yard. Try as he might to step out of the way, Ibrahim was knocked down by the first, furious soldiers and trampled underfoot. Kicked by every soldier that passed, his poor body was mangled beyond recognition. His eyes, gazing in surprise, were all that remained of Khaja Ibrahim Agha. Like a fish, his mouth opened and closed, but no breath came out.

Sayyah the Sorcerer made the best of what had befallen Ibrahim for his own ends. He tore the child from his mother who gazed at him in hopeless entreaty, dashed to the opposite corner, unrolled his prayer mat, took his red hat from his bundle, put it on, hid the child, silent from fright, in his broad robes, and entered his time of solitude with the child, forgetting all that was going on around him. He clutched the child firmly to his chest, his mouth against his heart so that if he did cry out they would be muffled by the beating of Sayyah's heart.

The soldiers stopped for a moment to stare at the tall,

smooth-cheeked dervish, who was chanting as he rocked back and forth, heedless of what was going on around him. Then they turned away from him and poured like a mountain stream into the house, pursuing the Caravanbashi's wife who was screaming as she tried to flee. An archer fell to one knee, took aim and shot his arrow. It hit her in the back and came out through her chest. She fell face down, her hair cascading out from her scarf like a waterfall, her green eyes closed. In a moment, she felt no more.

The soldiers charged into the big room and bent over the Caravanbashi's sprawling body. One of them drew his sharp sword, cut off the Caravanbashi's head with a crunch, put it in a sack and tied it up, ready to throw it at the Shah's feet. After furiously kicking the headless body, one of the soldiers suddenly shouted "that's enough" and looked around.

"What's happened to the child? He had a young son, didn't he? Find him!"

They spread out and walked through that great house, searched every inch of the servants' quarters across the yard, promising, "If you've hidden him, we'll crush the lot of you." But the child had disappeared into the earth like crumbs, or been drawn into the seventh heaven that cast its blinding light over the pure white snow that lay all around. The dervish was not to be seen either; he was no longer in the yard. He had vanished.

The snow that began that morning did not fall in flakes but in great balls. Nothing could be seen clearly, not houses, roads, trees, or people. Clutching the child, Sayyah rushed through the city, not pausing to rest. His eyes were closed, but he did not stumble or trip once, as though he had been travelling this way a thousand years. He surprised himself at his route. He did not travel a straight path, but twisted and turned. Maybe he was remembering his childhood in the Wheel of Fate?

He reached the city gates on the Pipes Road unseen by anyone. He was so out of breath his heart was almost in his mouth. The child had his soft arms around Sayyah's neck and was hugging his body to him so tightly that Sayyah was almost numb. He did not know where he found the strength to carry a child of that size. He did not want to think about it, fearing that if he did the strength would leave him.

The city gates had just opened. Weary wayfarers who had spent a frozen night at the closed city gates brought with them the frosty air of the plain as they walked slowly and sleepily into the city.

His head bowed, Sayyah walked past the guards who stared hard at him, and without looking at anyone walked out of the city. Then, without looking back, set out on the plain road at the same speed and in the same circuitous fashion. He felt in his heart that the soldiers would eventually come after him. He travelled a good way before his strength ran out and he had to stop for a rest. He wanted to put the child down but the boy stuck to him like tar. Holding the child, Sayyah looked back towards the city for the first time. The city and its great gates were slowly dissolving in the whiteness. Were anyone looking in their direction from the city, they would see only a white statue. Soon this whiteness, invisible even to each other, moved off again.

Before setting out again, Sayyah looked back once more towards the city but could not see it at all. The city was no more, as if it had turned into a huge snow-white mountain. Sayyah blinked several times and stared again at the city, remembering the words many years ago of the Yellow Sayid, and was sure that at that moment the city was no more.

The frost began to bite. Sayyah wrapped himself in his scarcely perceptible shadow in the grey, frozen earth. With the child in his arms, he turned his back on the city that was no more and continued on his way.

CHAPTER 20
Eternal Spring in the Valley of the Sorcerers

The blizzard raging around the Invisible Mountain was of no concern in the Valley of the Sorcerers. The road that skirted the foot of the Invisible Mountain was smothered in white. The whole world seemed to have turned into a white shroud.

It was spring again in the Valley of the Sorcerers. Flower called to flower, nightingale to nightingale. Groups of sorcerers were busy talking, one group strolling through the valley, another sitting on the green sward around a rose bush. Only the White Dervish, his heart uneasy, his thoughts brooding far away, could hear the ragged breath and rhythmic beating of an approaching heart. He already knew whose heart it was that was beating, before the image of Sayyah appeared before his eyes and did not go away. He also saw the child in his arms and, behind them, the city that was no more, swathed in white mist.

His heart could wait no longer and he set out on the road winding up out of the valley. He walked slowly along the road until he reached the head of the valley. He could not go any further. If he left the valley, a hole would open up the size of the distance he had travelled, and through that hole would come cold and frost from the world outside. The sorcerers had had to come together and use all their strength to stop the hole left by Sayyah. The White Dervish would have to wait. The beating of Sayyah's heart and his ragged breathing were already very close. At this moment, voices came to the White Dervish from one of those worlds, from one of those yards. The voices mingled, and this time an ancient vision came to life before him.

"Truly, everything is only a moment. Everything is within this moment, the past and the future." Those words were spoken by the venerable master, Sheikh Manuchohr ibn Sadiq, two young disciples sitting opposite him, two inseparable friends clasping each other's hands as they sat side by side.

"That moment does not exist for me, because this moment does not yet have a name." Those words were spoken by one of the young disciples who was called the Yellow Sayid.

"Whether that moment has a name or not is of no concern to me; I can see it in my heart," said the White Dervish.

The Sheikh smiled. "It already has a name! Its name is the full moment. The full moment has gathered everything within itself, the past and the future."

Stroking his long white beard, Sheikh Manuchohr screwed up his eyes and looked tenderly and rather sadly at the two young men.

The White Dervish carefully received the child, who had found sanctuary in sleep, from Sayyah the Sorcerer's exhausted hands, and began to walk down the green path into the eternal spring of the Valley of the Sorcerers, carefully watching his every step. His knees trembling from weariness, Haji Mir Hasan Agha

Sayyah—Sayyah the Sorcerer—staggered after him, brushing off the now melting snow.

If you loved this book, please provide
a review at Amazon.com?

CPSIA information can be obtained at www.ICGtesting.com
Printed in the USA
BVOW05s0817051115

425847BV00001B/7/P